MANBORG

BRET NELSON

BASED ON THE SCREENPLAY BY

STEVEN KOSTANSKI AND JEREMY GILLESPIE

CONTENTS

FOREWORD

BY STEVEN KOSTANSKI

My cinema obsession has always included the culture that spawns from movies, specifically the tie-in merchandise that came with the most iconography-laden genre films. Toys, videogames, comics, soap (I have a bar of *Phantom Menace* soap with a little Darth Maul bust buried inside it still in the pack somewhere) - all of it informs the universes created by these movies. A *Terminator 2* arcade game? A *Hellraiser* thermos? A *Dune* (1984) colouring book? Sure, why not!

So when Mark Miller approached me about licensing my dollar-store sci-fi epic *Manborg* for a novelization, my heart said "yes" before I even finished reading the email. How could I turn him down when I had a copy of the *Ghostbusters 2* novelization staring at me from the shelf?

Bret Nelson has transformed my admittedly simplistic film script into an engaging action-packed story, expanding the world and the characters in an organic way that typically doesn't happen with novels adapted from feature films. His passion for the material bleeds into every page, making it a very infectious read full of heart and humour. I couldn't put it down once I started reading it, and this is coming from the guy who spent 3 years buried in this story and was more than happy to never experience it again.

It's a great companion piece to the film, and I'm honored to have the talented folks at Encyclopocalypse inject some fresh life into the undead cyborg that is *MANBORG*.

Steven Kostanski

May 2022

PROLOGUE

THE HELL WARS

At 11:32 AM ON APRIL 8TH, 1987, THE INFERNO GATE OPENED, AND the Hell Wars began.

Hell's first assault lasted 93 minutes and killed a third of Earth's population. That assault would have kept going, but every one of Hell's forces paused to gorge on the blood of the dead.

Ten minutes later, they picked up where they left off and killed just about everyone else.

The Bible speaks of the end. Of Angels pouring bowls of God's wrath into the seas and rivers - turning them into blood.

That's pretty close to what happened, except instead of Angels it was foot soldiers of the damned. And instead of bowls they carried every weapon ever made.

There was no build up, no warning, no rising sound of chaos. The gate between Earth and the Abyss opened and Hell was here. The demons and their soulless troops were everywhere all at once. Within the first few seconds, that gate became a ragged laceration across the whole planet. A world-splitting gash, ripping at the edges as every damned thing clawed out and started killing.

And feeding.

They looked nearly human, at a distance. Most of them had limbs, and something like a head. They moved oddly, some shambling, others darting from place to place. Some even flew.

But all of them had mouths. And teeth. And guns.

Every means of communication stopped working as soon as they arrived. No phones, no news. All anyone could do was scream and hope somebody heard.

Anything people counted on like the police or the army failed utterly and collapsed under the same wave that destroyed everything else. And by the end of the third day, it was over. Can anything 72 hours long be called a "war?"

On that last day, a leader rose from the Abyss, assigned to rule Hell on Earth.

Count Draculon.

A demon, with supernatural powers. He was eight feet tall, with grey, leathery skin, sunken eyes, long hair, and a resonant voice that came from all around like a church bell. He leapt great distances, nearly flying. Some said he moved objects with his thoughts.

And like the forces he controlled, he drank blood. Gallons of it, but he wasn't a vampire. He had no weakness. The sun didn't harm him, it didn't even make him squint. He ignored holy water, crosses, garlic, and wooden stakes. The people who tried to use them became a quick meal. Bullets and grenades were equally ineffective.

He had a second-in-command called The Baron. His skin and eyes were similar to those of his master, but he was shorter, hairless, and had a mouth filled with needle-like teeth. He wore a full-length, black leather jacket, like one of Hitler's lieutenants.

The Baron may have been a high-ranking member of the Abwehr before his arrival in Hell. Or maybe he was one of the U.S. Cavalry's enforcers at the Powder River War. Or any of Caligula's favorite senators.

Or maybe he was just another demon. It didn't really matter. What did matter was that Hell was creating a structure. A method of rule. They were going to be here for a long time.

Draculon announced himself to the world with a quiet show of strength. He appeared simultaneously on every screen and speaker on the planet. Phones, laptops, monitors, televisions, video billboards, and car radios all lit with his image and voice. It took everyone by surprise, as none of these had worked for days.

He spoke, and all the armies of Hell stood still.

"I am Count Draculon, and I require your silence."

Everything, all around the world, went quiet. Even the screaming.

"You have been annexed. Hell is here. All that you once knew is part of the Abyss now. From this point forward, my armies will stop attacking."

There were people who took those words, took that moment as an opportunity to strike back at the Hellish forces. Those people were instantly shredded.

"Of course," said Draculon, "my armies will continue to defend themselves.

"I know what you are wondering, here in your most desperate hours. You wonder, 'where are the Angels? Where are the armies of Heaven to fight the armies of Hell?' The answer is simple: The Angels are not coming. We are not at war with Heaven. We have no quarrel with them. They do not have what we want.

"You do. You have blood. We are no longer attackers. We are gatherers. Please, come out from where you are hiding. Come out and greet my troops. They will take you, peacefully.

"They will take you to a place where your fate is assured. Go with them and find peace."

Those who cooperated were taken to processing centers and camps. They were allowed to live but drained of their blood at a manageable rate. Those who were strong enough were forced to build Hell on Earth.

Of course, some resisted. The only humans that evaded death or capture were either very good at hiding or very good at killing. A few excelled at both. So, from their newly established capitals, Hell's generals created hunters.

This new wave of damned soldiers was augmented with Hell-tech. Each of the soulless became a tangle of skin and weapons and wires. They called them "Killborgs," and armed them with guns of the future. They wore uniforms of black and red, with a jagged insignia slashing a white circle on each arm.

Hell didn't need an upgrade; their victory was assured. They made the Killborgs because they could, and the excruciating augments were a new way to punish the damned.

1 / THE SWEET TASTE OF HOPE

THE WIND BIT MIKE HALLORAN'S FACE. THE COLD WAS WORSE UP HERE on top of the water tower. "It's been six months, Bro," he said. "Six months to the day since that dickhead Draculon said they weren't going to attack anymore." Another gust forced him to bury his nose in his shoulder.

His brother, Wayne, ignored him as he scanned the ruins of the street below through the scope of his rifle. "Call me 'Sir' or 'Sarge,'" he said. "You've got to make that a habit."

"Yes, Sir." Mike stooped and dug through his kit bag, searching for ammunition. "Those training sessions wasted a lot of bullets," he said. "We've only got fifteen rounds left."

He waited for a response as he watched Wayne slide down on one knee, resting the gun's barrel on the tower's rail.

"Did you hear me? Yesterday, when we worked with Rachel's group, we used too much ammo on target practice," said Mike.

Wayne said nothing. Staring through the scope, he lined up on a lone Killborg scout. He squeezed the trigger and the Killborg's head lolled over as sparks and a spatter of ichor hit the wall behind it.

"I disagree," said Wayne, watching the Killborg fall. "Besides, I traded the last of our live rounds with Rachel. Those are all blanks."

"What?!" Mike held one of the bullets up close, staring at the ends.

"Just messing with you," said Wayne. "Have you checked the mail?"

"Hang on, Bro - I mean, Sir," said Mike. With half a smile, he dropped the bullet back in the bag and pulled out a worn set of binoculars. He peered down the street to the burned-out remnants of a liquor store. In the one remaining window, a poster of a bikini-clad girl beckoned soccer fans to drink beer. The poster was hung sideways.

"West," said Mike. "Rendezvous is that football stadium west of here."

"That means Donna's squad found survivors. Let's go."

————

Mike and Wayne Halloran had been serving in the Canadian Rangers together for two years before Hell came to Earth. Wayne, a sergeant, had been there longer. He convinced Mike, his kid brother, to sign on shortly after his eighteenth birthday.

"You'll love this," Wayne told him. "It's like a wilderness run that never ends. We're always ready to help people, but no one lives here."

"Here" was Nunavut, and Wayne was right. There were less than 40,000 people in the 750,000 square kilometer region. Most of them were isolated in one town, Iqaluit, on the tip of the Koojesse Inlet.

The Rangers' job was to patrol and protect the vast territory and its people. Mostly they camped and traveled. For all its size and rough terrain, Nunavut was an uneventful place.

Until the Inferno Gate opened back in April. The moment it happened, the squad's sat radio and phones stopped working, like the rest of the communication gear on the planet. Per protocols, they decided to make their way to Iqaluit. Once there, they'd get the equipment checked out and contact Command.

Soon, it became clear there was more going on than a communications glitch. From their temporary camp in the Everett

Mountains, they heard screams and gunfire echoing off the canyons and ridges. Smoke rose on the horizon. Hell's raiding parties had reached all the way to this remote spot in the north.

Sergeant Wayne Halloran oversaw three other Rangers. Donna Campbell got her first sharpshooting trophy at the age of ten. She had a pale complexion and dark hair, but you never saw them because she was always bundled up against the cold. Knit caps and gaiters framed her green eyes.

Rudy Polaris grew up on a farm in Alberta. He was immune to cold, wearing board shorts in the snow. He said his mop of bright, orange hair kept him warm.

And Mike Halloran was Wayne's kid brother. They were just a few years apart, but Wayne looked much older than Mike. That was only because Mike looked so much younger than his actual age.

The weather and terrain in this, Canada's most severe region, had given them a preview of Hell on Earth, making them durable people.

It took two days to get out of the mountains and reach town. The shooting and screams had stopped the night before. The stench of death and burned skin kept coming.

By the time they got into Iqaluit, Hell's army had moved on. The town was burning. Hollowed-out bodies littered every street. There were no survivors.

The power was working. Lights were on. Smoke and security alarms wailed. But phones, computers, televisions, anything that could connect the Rangers with anyone else was down.

As they searched the rubble for explanations, video and audio spontaneously sparked onto every screen. The Rangers watched Draculon's announcement on cracked displays in what was once a sports bar.

"That guy," said Donna, "this is all real, isn't it? The rest of the world is like this, in ruins, and everybody's dead?"

"Not everybody," said Wayne. "They missed us, and we can't be the only ones."

"I'm going to find a higher vantage," said Donna, "I want to see if there's any trouble coming." She did a quick check on her rifle and sidearm, then headed out.

"I wonder what all is left of Dunn's," said Rudy. Wayne and Mike lit up.

"We need to get there right now," said Mike.

All three of the men moved quick but quiet across the three blocks to Dunn's Guns. Terrance Dunn's store had been in business for more than fifty years and was well stocked.

The building was barely standing, but there was no fire. That was a good sign.

Inside, there was ordinance scattered everywhere.

"This is terrible," said Mike.

"This is beautiful," said Rudy.

"We need a van," said Wayne.

"The creeps are about 5 kilometers out of town, heading toward Cape Dorset," said Donna. No one heard her come in.

"How did you know we were here?" asked Mike.

"I didn't. I just wanted guns. Have you guys looked out back?"

They moved past the aisles and into the storage room. The rear wall of the building was gone. Death and bullet holes were everywhere. Many of the bodies weren't human.

"The people must have made their stand here," said Mike. "Makes sense, plenty to fight with right there in the store."

"But look at what they were fighting," said Rudy. "These things, they aren't people. They're like the one on T.V., twisted and weird."

"From Hell," said Wayne. "That's what he said. Count Draculon said we are at war with Hell. At least we know they can be killed."

"Look at their mouths," said Mike. "Red all around, dripping off their chins. It's the only blood I've seen. All those dead people, all those bodies, and no blood. Were these things feeding?"

"We need to get out of here," said Donna. "Let's get some transport."

Back in the street, it didn't take long to find a promising vehicle. The work van was on its side, but it was in one piece. It had front and rear seating in the cabin and a big cargo area. The logo on the side read "Admiral Boat Repair," with an image of the Admiral himself. He looked too old for the hotties in sailor togs hanging off each of his arms.

The squad rocked the beastly thing back and forth. On the third try it rolled over onto its wheels, but it made a terrible racket. Everyone disappeared into the surrounding rubble and listened for trouble.

A call echoed through the streets. A screech, big, as if it came from an enormous, injured hawk. Silence for a moment, then a different call. This one was lower in pitch, but it still made everyone's teeth clench.

"What is that?" asked Rudy.

"Gotta be those things," said Wayne. "We need to get clear."

Donna started toward an office building across the street. "I got on that roof pretty easy earlier. Let's go."

All followed Donna with their rifles slung across their backs. They moved slow and careful until another set of calls rang out, then everyone sprinted. She was right about access being simple, a hop on a dumpster then up the fire escape. The building hadn't taken much damage in the prior assault, so the roof was stable, and a short railing ran the perimeter. It didn't provide much cover, but if they kept low, they'd be tough to spot.

Another pair of shrieks drew everyone's attention to the south. Two creatures stood at an intersection four blocks away. They stayed there a moment, then came walking up the street, getting closer, speaking in rasping chatters at each other.

"Look at them. So ugly," said Rudy. "Scales and hair and spines."

"And they're armed," said Donna.

"Yeah, some sort of modified assault rifles," said Mike, peering through his binoculars. "It looks like they're talking to each other. Is that even possible?"

The beasts reached another intersection and stopped. They looked up and down all the streets, then took turns making the long, loud cries the Rangers heard before. After they called out, the beasts stood still, listening.

"They're waiting for an answer," said Wayne. When no answer came, the creatures resumed their heated chattering and moved up the street. The smaller one punched the larger one in the chest.

"They're lost," said Donna. "They got left behind. Now they can't find their way and they're arguing about it." At the next corner, the pair called out again.

Rudy aimed his rifle, the barrel below the railing. "It's a clear shot," he said.

"Wait until they're in front of that mailbox," said Wayne, readying his weapon. "Mike, you take the big guy. I'll aim for him, too. Donna, Rudy, you're on the little one."

"Set," said Donna.

"You call it," said Rudy.

The four of them waited as the Hell-born pair made their way up the street. "Ten more steps," Wayne said. "Line up. On three, keep shooting until they drop. Then a couple more rounds to make sure. Careful not to cross each other."

When the beasts reached the mailbox, Wayne counted off, and all four of the Rangers' Colt rifles started popping. Every bullet found its target, and it took a few moments for the creatures to realize they were being fired on. By the time they got their weapons up, they'd each been hit more than a dozen times. They fell, and Wayne said, "hold."

There was no movement from the creatures. Everyone lowered their rifles and smiled. Rudy started to speak, but Mike stopped him and whispered, "That was noisy. We should listen for a minute, make sure we're clear."

They held still for a few minutes and heard nothing but the wail of the alarms.

"Clear," said Rudy. "Let's get going."

"That took a lot of bullets," said Donna, climbing down the fire escape. "We've got to aim better. Maybe try to focus on headshots."

The rangers returned to the Admiral's van. "Tank's full, and the keys are here, but that tire's had it," said Mike.

Donna was clearing out the cargo area. "There's no spare," she called.

A single, far-off burst of gunfire interrupted their analysis.

"There's no time to find something better," said Wayne. "We'll have to ride the rim. Let's load all the guns and ammo we can. I'm thinking we use that fire road along the river."

"You mean the one that goes to Grinnell Park? That's a good idea," said Rudy.

"The park is huge," said Wayne. "Once we're in there, we can stow this shit and hide at any of the stations. We can maybe rest a bit and get a plan together. And we can buy a hot dog at the snack bar."

"No way it's still open, look around you," said Mike. The others laughed.

"Just messing with you," said Wayne.

They loaded the van as fast as possible without making a lot of noise. The engine started on the first try. Mike drove while the rest kept their heads on swivels. The flat tire made it slow going, especially once they made it to the fire road.

The truck shook over a rut and lurched to the left, tipping slightly and threatening to fall into the river. Wayne grabbed the wheel, helping Mike keep the teetering wreck centered.

"Dammit Mike! I know it's a crap road but it's the only one there is. Stay to the right!"

"Yeah," said Donna, looking out her window to the churning water below. "Force it over or we'll have a splashdown."

"The tire on this side is flat," said Mike. "You know it's flat. And I'm pretty sure the back axle is busted. I can't really steer this pig. I can only ... influence it."

"Well, influence it to the right," said Wayne. "We just have to make it over that rise up ahead, another couple of kilometers."

The grinding of the truck's power train slowly devouring itself was the only sound anyone heard for a time.

"I'll bet there's others like us," said Mike. "We should look for other people and get organized."

Over the following six months, they pushed south, becoming the most successful resistance group on this continent.

———

Today, they were in southern Manitoba, outside of what used to be Brandon, making their way to the old United States border. The Killborgs were spread thin through here. There wasn't enough blood to motivate them.

Earth's population was five billion before the initial attack. By the time Count Draculon announced Hell's rule, that number had shrunk to 20 million.

Wayne's Rangers, as they came to be known, had grown to more than a hundred people, working their way cross country in tight squads of five or six. They were making parts of the colder north into tiny safe zones for survivors.

With posters on ruined buildings, flags, and notes in dead drops, a crude communication network formed. They freed survivors from the Killborg encampments and set up places for people to hide. So far, more than 2,000 escapees found hope in the Ranger-maintained safe zones.

If anyone could fight, they were recruited. The rookies hungered for vengeance, wanted to take out all the Killborgs they saw. Squashing that rage was the first part of their training.

"Forget about killing all the Killborgs," Wayne would tell them. "If every bullet in the world scored a perfect headshot, that would only eliminate about ten percent of the bastards. We can't wipe them out. But we can remove a few pinpointed guards, and free people. That's a victory. Every person we save is a win. Our family is growing.

"That's how you keep score. Don't count how many Killborgs you take down. Count how many people you take away from them. It's not about the killing. It's about family."

Later that afternoon, they met up with Donna and her squad at the stadium. They had ten civilian refugees with them.

Donna and Wayne exchanged updates. She was taking her group to The Crossing; an old rail stop that served as a secret outpost for the resistance. She would meet up with Rudy's squad there and they'd escort the refugees to the Riding Mountain Safe Zone.

"We should go along, too," said Mike. "Maybe we can get more ammo at The Crossing."

"I don't know," said Wayne. "We should be pushing further south. Supposed to hook up with Ted's people at the border in three days."

"Oh, come on," said Mike. "It's not that far out of the way. Please Sarge?"

———

By early the next morning, all of them, including Mike and Wayne, arrived at The Crossing. It consisted of a dead rail line, what used to be a storage building with a platform, and a rotting water tower. The building gave shelter and stored gear.

The day was unseasonably warm. They could smell the grass. And there were plenty of bullets.

"Bro, how long has it been since we heard birds?" asked Mike, packing his kit bag with full magazines.

"Don't call me 'Bro,'" said Wayne, loading his rifle and sidearm. "It's important to keep things sharp."

"Right. So, Sarge, do you hear the birds?"

"Yes. It's nice."

"It's hopeful," said Donna.

Everyone took a moment to breathe in the air. And listen.

There was another sound on the wind. Booming.

"Thunder?" asked Donna.

Thirty meters away, part of the landscape exploded.

"Hell's thunder," said Wayne. "Donna, your people got anything heavy?"

"Hey Corey," called Donna, "bring that RPG up front!"

"Excellent," said Wayne. "Get those refugees back. Everybody else form up on me and dig in!"

Turning a slow circle, Mike tried to see the entire world through his binoculars.

"Mike - where are they?" asked Rudy. His squad had come running from the shelter to join the line. That made fifteen Rangers, armed and ready.

"Can't see anything ... crap, scratch that, I found them," Mike said. "Bro, southwest, just the other side of that wrecked billboard. Coming fast, you see them?"

"Don't call me Bro,'" said Wayne. "And yes, everyone sees them."

So many. In front was a company of Boners, oversized skeleton monsters with round grenade launchers implanted at the end of each arm.

Behind them, teams of Killborgs worked two enormous flame cannons, each carried smoothly on hovering platforms. Poles in the rear of both platforms supported immense flags with the Killborg insignia on a bright field of red.

The rest of the battalion was made up of Killborg foot soldiers with pulse guns.

None of that was a problem. Wayne's crew had dealt with worse. The problem was the pair in front of the Boners. Striding at an unfeasible pace over the rough terrain was The Baron, barking orders. To his right was a taller figure, with a cape and heavy boots. Long hair and grey skin. Unmistakable.

Count Draculon was leading this assault. They were walking straight for The Crossing, which was clearly no longer a secret location.

That meant the safe zones were no longer safe.

"Fuck me," said Wayne. "Rudy!"

"Yeah, Sarge?"

"Get moving, fast. Fall back and spread the word. Hell found us.

Everyone needs to bug out and find new places to be. We have to assume every position is compromised."

"Sarge, I can't get to everyone."

"Just get to Riding Mountain, it's the closest and they can spread the word from there."

"Holy shit!" said Mike. The advancing Hell corps were already less than 100 meters away. They had closed an impossible distance. Draculon let his troops march past him as he laughed.

"Hold the line!" called Wayne. "Rudy, get those people out of here!"

Bolts from the Killborg pulse guns and bullets from the Rangers' Colt assault rifles were flying everywhere.

"Cover Fire! Get these Killborgs off my ass!" said Wayne.

"Yeah, Bro!" said Mike. "I mean - Sir!"

Mike tried to concentrate, but he couldn't hit a thing. He felt himself stressing when he heard Wayne call to him again.

"It's okay man," said Wayne. "Just chill out. Pick your shots and stay focused!"

"Ok! Yeah!" Mike slowed down, held his breath, and his next trigger-pulls took down two of the crew running a flame cannon. The platform carrying it went nose-down into the turf as the weapon fired wildly into the surrounding Killborgs. As a group of them tried to right the thing, the whole rig exploded. Mike had taken down nineteen enemies with two shots.

The rest of the Hell corps marched past the wreckage, ignoring it.

Wayne spotted Corey behind a rubble pile with the RPG on his shoulder. He was looking for the thickest grouping of targets. Wayne jumped over the pile to join him.

"Your name's Corey, right?"

"Yes, Sir."

"Single target, Corey. Just hit Draculon."

"Really?"

"Fucking do it," said Wayne. "Plant it right in his chest if you can."

"Yes, Sir." As Corey lined up the shot, Draculon turned his gaze to Wayne.

Draculon stood unblinking as the rocket left the launcher and sailed toward him. He never broke eye contact as three Boners leapt across the field and swallowed the rocket for their master. They were destroyed, he was untouched.

At that point, Wayne's rage overshadowed his reason. "Come and get it you assholes!"

He stood tall and emptied his Colt, then drew his sidearm and emptied that. Nearly every shot was a kill. That got the attention of The Baron, who in turn gave a signal to the crew on the remaining flame cannon. They launched a fireball that destroyed the rubble pile in front of Wayne and Corey. The force of the detonation got them airborne. Corey died mid-flight. Wayne hit the ground spitting up blood.

Mike saw the whole thing and ran to his brother. He was still alive, just.

"Talk to me," said Mike. "Tell me what I can do."

"Bro," said Wayne. "Get out."

"No! I can't leave you here!"

"We helped a lot of people. You're a good kid ..."

"No! You can't go!" Mike saw they only had seconds left together.

Rangers were falling dead left and right. The Killborgs were winning.

"Just ... remember," said Wayne. "It's not about the killing. It's about ... family"

He handed Mike a picture of the two of them together, in happier times. "Now run, that's an order." He stopped moving, stopped coughing.

Fighting his tears, Mike sprinted away. "Yes, Sir!"

As the Killborgs chased down Rudy's group, Draculon paused by Wayne's ravaged body. He stepped on the sergeant, and Wayne coughed up more blood.

"Still living? Even now, you resist," said Draculon.

"Go to Hell!" spat Wayne.

"Not yet," said Draculon, smiling. "But soon, I will bring Hell to you."

His great hands grabbed Wayne Halloran by his shoulders and lifted him off the ground. Draculon buried his face in Wayne's neck and tore it open. He gulped down all the blood, then tossed the body aside, his face smeared red.

"Oh," said Draculon. "They taste so much better when they still have hope."

Mike saw the whole thing. He charged, firing. Fury drove his aim to perfection. He ran at Draculon, taking out all the Killborgs along the way with bullets or the butt of his gun.

His attack was stopped by the sight of Draculon's massive sword swinging towards his head. With a quick duck, Mike avoided the blade and blocked the next blow with his rifle. With a feint to the left, Mike managed to fire a shot that glanced off Draculon's shoulder.

Even the Count was impressed, but it was time for this to be finished. He brought down his sword and split the rifle in half, then kicked Mike in the chest, sending him sailing ten meters where he bounced off a stack of old railroad ties.

As he tried to get up and continue the fight, pain tore through every bit of Mike Halloran. His spine was broken.

Draculon stood over him. "Such a shame," he said. "If only you weren't so fragile, then maybe we could've had a real fight."

Just as he had done with his brother, Draculon lifted Mike by his shoulders. The pain was immeasurable. "This isn't over!" shouted Mike. "I'm gonna get you and I'm gonna cut you to pieces!"

"Will you? I look forward to that," said Draculon. With one hand, he dangled Mike Halloran in front of his Killborgs, a living target. In unison, they fired their pulse guns. He died hanging from the demon's palm.

As Draculon dropped the corpse, The Baron approached cautiously with a report. "None here are alive," he said. "The man you drained; he was the one in charge. This guy was his brother, I think. Well done, my Lord."

"Baron, stop sucking up. It grates on me," said Draculon.

"Oh … well, no more sucking then. I'll just call in the Bloodscrappers and we'll get the last bits out of these guys. Yup. I am doing that now."

———

Hours later, the screams and gunfire in the distance subsided and the sound of birds returned. A party of Bloodscrappers arrived to wring the final drops of plasma out of the dead. They had no way of knowing that Mike Halloran's body had gone missing.

2 / A HERO MADE OF HELL-TECH

CERTAIN BEINGS IMPRINT ON THINGS AT BIRTH, LIKE A PARENT'S FACE OR a spawning location. This is well documented, and any biology textbook will confirm it. But there is another, more recent discovery: Humans sometimes imprint on things at death.

To be clear, this was a recent discovery on Earth. It's been known in Hell for eons.

Mike Halloran's final actions, thoughts, and feelings were singular: Destroy Count Draculon. Rage, vengeance, and fury pounded through every cell and neuron with no outlet.

Many other people had used their last moments to spout loathing at Draculon, but not like this. Halloran charged at him and attacked first with bullets, then used his rifle as a club. With his last breath, even as the Killborg weapons tore him apart, he screamed his vow to annihilate the Count.

That energy, those final brain signals, were still inside him. Even though he was dead, the imprint remained. A devout person would say he was a vessel for an angry spirit or tortured soul.

That imprint became the core of Mike Halloran's new form.

In an old warehouse, thirty kilometers from the field where he died, Halloran's wrecked corpse lay hidden. He'd been brought there in secret so he could save the world.

And the work began.

A micro-compressor pumped preservative stabilizers through his veins, replacing the blood and sealing wounds along the way.

Robotic pincers swapped out his muscle groups for actuated tension polymers, the outermost layer matching his skin.

His retooled circulatory system ran on a fixed network of vitality fibers.

Hell-tech weapons filled spaces once occupied by bones, with a truss of rigid nano-struts supporting the heavier guns.

Exo-skeletal armor guarded the key systems and circuitry that tied it all to his brain. Rage would drive his actions.

Memory, dreams, and feelings might carry over into his new existence, but there was no way to be certain until he woke. That would be a decade from now.

Halloran's vengeance had to wait. Draculon's victory was not yet complete. The Count was agitated, still on guard. But once Hell's rule was established and things got quiet, an opportunity might arise.

A hero might have a chance then. So, the new Mike Halloran was crated and hidden under the streets on the outskirts of Hell's growing capital, Meganet City. The liquefied Amrita Life Source installed in his chest would keep him stable. The timer on his main systems would trigger a full power-up in ten years.

3 / THE GRIND

Just before his cabin in America's western desert was overrun by Killborgs, Chad Woolridge was updating his notes. In the ten years since Hell's arrival, the cultural anthropologist had been living here unseen, documenting the human race's subjugation.

As the first Killborg's blade pushed through his back and out his chest, blood spread over the color-coded timeline on his worktable. The chart had blue boxes outlining the rise and defeat of the resistance forces and their so-called "safe zones" over the first two years of the war. Gray lines connected some of those boxes to the purple trapezoids tracing the 5-year history of *Puño de la Humanidad* in the northern region of Colombia.

This collective of criminals, powerbrokers, and their private armies created a fortress covering most of Antioquia. For a time, they turned Hell away. But at the end of their fifth year, everything south of Panama and north of Caldas fell into the sea.

Eight minutes of rumbling.

Of churning rock and lava.

The ocean became steam.

It was still after that. South America had a new and different coastline and *Puño de la Humanidad* was gone.

After that, the only fortresses left in the world were the vast cities built for Hell's regime. There was one on every continent, and each spread over most of the land.

After another Killborg's blade swung through his neck, Chad's headless body slumped forward and dumped gore over the binders containing his personal journals. Here, he wrote about how quickly humanity adjusted to Hell's rule, and how sad it made him. Even before the resistance forces fell, most people had accepted their fate and moved into the dense, filthy cities. They agreed to give blood in exchange for their lives. The cities were mostly populated by the damned, humans were just a sliver of the inhabitants.

None lived well. And none fought back. No riots, no marches, no underground. Just obedience.

Chad's head bounced off the west wall, leaving a red, starburst pattern in the middle of a large map of Meganet City, in what used to be North America. It was Hell's capitol, and he'd been collecting information about the "Genesis Tower" at its center. It was a landmark facility for scientific advancement and entertainment. Chad's hand-written notations dotted the map, defining the "science" as human experimentation and the "entertainment" as human slaughter.

Bloodscrappers dragged what was left of Chad Woolridge to their cart and wrung out his remains. It took a Killborg Flame Crew fourteen minutes to burn the cabin and its contents to ash.

The heavy battles were long since over, and Hell was victorious, so The Baron was rewarded with a cushy administrative position. From his office in the Genesis Tower, he ran Meganet City.

He was a fierce warrior, but unlike Count Draculon, fighting never brought him pleasure. His current position didn't bring him much pleasure, either. Hosting the battles in the Terroropticon arena was the only thing that made the job tolerable.

The tower connected to a central complex where new weapons and creatures were created. Next door to that stood the

Terroropticon, an enormous stadium where humans battled those creatures and bled, thrilling Hell's denizens, and feeding them at the same time. Thinking about those arena fights helped push the rotten parts of the job out of his mind.

The Baron felt as if his eyes itched, but he knew that wasn't possible. His eyes were torn out a month ago. A pair of ocular implants restored his sight. The metallic red discs granted him better vision than his eyes ever did, but he still wasn't used to them.

Just another annoyance for a Thursday morning. He hated Thursdays. That was when he had to meet with humans who felt they had something to offer, and therefore they should be given special treatment. On rare occasions, one would prove useful to Hell's regime.

He'd seen more than a dozen so far today, and every one of them was worthless.

His final meeting was with a social media influencer, or rather, that's what she was, when there was social media. He read the forms Dorothy Singer had submitted. He listened to her jabber. Then he closed her folder and dropped it onto his desk. "Your proposition," said The Baron, "is pointless."

"That can't be." She tried to step forward, but The Baron's raised hand stopped her.

"Please. I've heard it all morning," he said. "We've made several options available for those who wish to live, but each comes with its own level of -- discomfort. So, thinking yourself unique, you strut in here and offer me a deal I don't need."

"But I had so many followers," said Dolores. "Millions of people were on my social media channels, and they'll do anything I tell them." She leaned in and whispered, "If you let me reach out to them, they will come running to furnish blood. Many will give all they have."

"Obedient blood is weak. It's blood-light," said The Baron. "Nearly flavorless and the hunger returns too soon. I have no use for the blood of your followers."

"But you're always telling people to give blood. It's on every screen in the city. Aren't those volunteers obedient?"

"Yes, and it's good enough to feed our Hellborn masses. They like it just fine. But that's my point … we have all the docile blood we need." The Baron waved toward a row of kegs against the wall. "Those are filled with fighting blood, the blood of resourceful combatants. That is rich blood. It satisfies."

The Baron leaned across his desk. "So, can you fight? Or train fighters?"

"No."

"Maybe some other skill … are you an engineer? Or a surgeon? Can you make my Killborgs more efficient?"

"No."

The Baron was puzzled. "Why did all those people follow you?"

"I helped them make decisions about shopping."

"I see," said The Baron. He called to the Killborg in the hall. "Take her back to the draining queue."

Dolores Singer planted her feet as the Killborg grabbed her arm. "Please, not that. I was brave enough to ask for this meeting. Doesn't that set me apart? Doesn't that earn me some kind of favor?"

The Baron considered this for a moment. "Let her cut to the front of the line," he said. The Killborg led Singer out and another took its place in the hall.

A hoverbot floated into the office. Its tin voice reported, "you have no more human appointments."

"Finally, some good news. Go wait in the hall with GX 218."

"I'm GK 237, Baron," said the Killborg in the hall.

"Whatever," said The Baron as he searched through the heaps of papers and files covering his desk. He gained frustration and speed with every pile he moved. Finally, he pushed the whole lot onto the floor.

"Get in here!" he called. The Killborg hustled in, the hoverbot following close behind. "Not you!" The hoverbot returned to the hall as The Baron addressed the Killborg. "Take all this crap and burn it,"

As the Killborg started piling papers and files, The Baron continued his search, slamming each drawer that failed him until he finally found his quarry, a pack of Percheron Black cigarettes.

"There you are," he said, smiling. "Hid you so well I nearly lost you guys." The Killborg stopped working and stared at The Baron. "Don't give me that look. I'm still quitting. This is my last pack ever. There's nine more in here and then I'm done."

The hoverbot glided in again. "You wanted me to remind you to speak with Doctor Scorpius."

"Get out!"

————

A bank of monitors enveloped the east wall of the lab. The thirty-seven screens each running independent video feeds with sound. The smallest was the size of a notebook. The larger ones could conceal a refrigerator. They were a constant source of undulating light and colliding noise.

It made concentration impossible for Doctor Scorpius, a human in Hell's employ. Before the Inferno Gate opened, he was a leader in nano technology and genetics. Now, he used those skills to create better Killborgs and other tools.

All his screens flashed an image of The Baron. An automated voice announced, "The Baron is calling," and kept repeating it.

Doctor Scorpius dropped the tiny bit of circuitry he'd been working on and reached for his crutch. When he started working for The Baron, he'd asked for better safety protocols. After a series of lab accidents ruined his spine and legs, he finally got them.

He used a combination of Earth-tech and Hell-tech to allow him to walk again, but he still needed the crutch. An interface on his wrist let him adjust his nerve actuators and medication implants if the pain became severe.

The intercom was on the wall across the room. Once he got there and pressed the TALK button, he made a mental note to move the thing closer to his workstation.

"Yes?" said Doctor Scorpius.

"I need you here," said The Baron. "Bring everything you've got on the Shadow Project."

"You have everything. I had it sent over this morning. You should have a green binder labeled 'Shadow Project.'"

"Don't argue! Just bring it. Remember, Doctor Scorpius, the day you are viewed as anything but useful will be the day you enter the Terroropticon to face one of your creations."

It took twenty minutes for Doctor Scorpius to gather all the printouts and make his way through the building. He passed a Killborg walking from The Baron's office. It carried a precarious stack of files and papers, including a green binder labeled "Shadow Project."

Doctor Scorpius struggled with his crutch and his files as he maneuvered through the door. "Hello Doctor," said The Baron. "Let's see what you've brought. Hope it's good, this morning has been a bitch." Scorpius handed over a one-sheet summary and piled the rest of the material in front of The Baron.

"You've been busy," said Doctor Scorpius. "This desk was heaping with work the last time I was here."

"What? Oh yes, finally cleared all of it." He pulled a cigarette from the pack and lit up as he reviewed the paper. "This does look promising."

"I thought you were -"

"I *am* quitting, there's only … shut up and top line this for me."

"Certainly," said Doctor Scorpius. "The Shadow-Mega prototype has been in operation for a month now. This replaces our Shadow-Mammoth and Shadow-Virulent concepts, as it combines the most successful elements of both. The Mammoth and Virulent prototypes have been transitioned into the arena, and Shadow-Mega is now the only command-level creature in the city, working with your hunter and strike groups."

"I've been working with a Shadow-Mega. She's very good. How many of these do we have?"

"One."

"What?"

"We must be *certain* the chimeric DNA can move between forms without losing stability or mutating. Shadow-Mega changes shape depending on the task at hand. She can appear human, allowing free movement among those she's been assigned to acquire or destroy. She can lead your monsters or turn into one. This mosaic of genetics and technology needs fierce testing before we begin mass production, and what's more, the last thing I need is for another Shadow to see this one as a threat."

Doctor Scorpius turned to a schematic page in the binder and pushed it across the desk to The Baron. "Shadow-Mega is capable of violence, mayhem, and complex thought. For this project to be successful, she needs more time operating in the field. She needs to take our commands as she, in turn, commands a subordinate force."

"Okay, okay, I get it," said The Baron. "One thing still concerns me. This time you've started with a human, not one of ours. Are you absolutely sure she will remain loyal to us?"

"I scraped out all the humanity and bleached what was left," said Doctor Scorpius. "Her mind was stripped down to the bare studs, and we built on top of it. Shadow-Mega operates solely on a mission level. Loyalty is all that's there."

BRIGHT LIGHTS PEPPERED EVERY BUILDING IN MEGANET CITY, YET THE streets were always dark. The banners flying the Killborg Insignia had their own lamps, as did the posters reading "OBEY" and "SUBMIT" and "GIVE BLOOD or die." Everything else stayed in perpetual night.

Roger Barris pretended to read the posters as he walked, keeping his face toward the wall. That way the scanning bots didn't see his features. But even with his back turned, he knew he stood out. Most of the pedestrians crowding the multi-level stride lanes and catwalks weren't human.

Each step was risky. He was making his way to the lower levels, sharing space with the endless stream of hover vehicles racing by. The traffic never thinned out. Every hour was rush hour.

There were extra Killborg Cops on patrol today. Besides dodging the regular peacekeeping forces, he had to avoid the backup squads for the Blood Crew.

They made their rounds twice a month, every other Thursday here in Zone 17. The Blood Crew went door to door collecting one regulation container from each housing unit and dropping off an empty one to be filled for next time.

Every housing unit owed one liter of blood per resident in a big, Hell-provided jug. And someone had better be home to hand it over.

If the contributions were light or the blood was watered down, the Crew would drain whoever answered the door.

One liter per resident, right then and there, from whoever answered the door.

The Killborgs didn't ask where the blood came from. They didn't care if everyone in the unit donated equally. Some buildings held a lottery on every floor. Some people hunted the streets, looking for an involuntary lodger to supply their family's portion.

Today, Roger Barris had run out of time. He didn't have a third of what he owed. For months, the ailing cousin who shared his unit had been supplying all the blood. She died last week.

Barris hoped to find a new roommate to strap into the drip machine in his back closet, where he kept his cousin. But no one answered the ad. Maybe people were getting wise to this sort of scam.

The Crew was moving through his building now. He made it to an alley on ground level and hid. No one came down here, humans were forbidden. Seated in a dark corner, he hoped it would all just go away.

———

One block over and ten meters down in the sewer, a dust-coated crate stirred for the first time in a decade.

The hum of electronics.

Motors buzzing.

A series of beeps.

The being inside the crate was Mike Halloran, once. That didn't occur to him as he woke. He saw only black. Then code, numbers scrolling upwards. Graphs with vital signs appeared and disappeared. Finally, a progress bar filled in as the words "SYSTEM ACTIVE" materialized in red. Only then did he realize his eyes were still closed.

Well, his real eye was closed, anyway. The left side of his face was mostly intact, a remnant of his humanity. The rest of his head was armored Hell-tech cybertronics, including the glowing sphere where his right eye used to be.

He opened his human eye.

The lights on his chest panel and armor lit the interior of the box with flashes of color, interfering with his vision. He tried to move, but there wasn't enough space. And as he shifted about, he heard clicks and the whirring of servos.

With a mix of instinct and programming he punched through the top of the crate and stood, destroying the container that had been his hiding place for ten years.

Every sound he made echoed. He was in a tunnel. As his head pivoted around, objects that triggered his image library highlighted in white.

The ceiling had runs of *PIPE*

Nearby, on the ground, was a *BUCKET*

There was a *LADDER* bolted into the wall. That one sparked a thought: *The ladder might be a way out of the tunnel.*

He walked toward it, but his steps were clumsy. He had three gyro-feedback regulators, one in each leg and another in his lower torso, and they needed time to self-calibrate. For now, balance would be a challenge.

Climbing the ladder went well, but there was a heavy metal lid blocking the way at the top. He meant to give it a nudge and test its weight, but the pneumatics in his forearm took over and the 120-kilo iron disc went flying.

The soundscape changed. Vehicles roaring. Neon buzzing. He made it onto street level but the things around him didn't process.

Movement.

Machines.

Signs.

Lights.

Too much information coming all at once. He saw a gap between two buildings that looked dark and quiet. His gait was still unsteady, but he managed to get there. From the shadows, he watched as cars and hoverbikes zoomed past. Above him, figures moved on the multi-tiered sidewalks.

His legs faltered and he ended up on his hands and knees, face toward the street. He saw his reflection in a puddle below. Part was familiar, part was mechanical. Like so many other things in this new place, he didn't understand what he was looking at.

At the far end of the alley, a hover-car with flashing lights and a piercing siren came to a stop. The futuristic vehicle had a familiar logo on its doors: The Killborg Insignia.

Memories flashed:

Flags.

Flame cannons.

Loss.

"Oh no!" he said. It was the first time he'd spoken out loud. His voice surprised him. Deeper than he expected. Was that reverb? No matter. He kept low and found cover.

A hoverbot floated out of the back of the vehicle with three armored Killborg Cops close behind. All of them bore the insignia. The hoverbot's faux voice repeated *Roger Barris ... Roger Barris* as its spotlight scanned the alley. The Killborgs knocked over boxes and debris, searching.

A moment before they reached his hiding place, Roger Barris stood with his hands over his head. "I'm Barris," he said. "Must have got my days mixed up."

"Hold him," the taller Killborg said. The other two each grabbed an arm as Barris winced from the pain. The hoverbot rotated a claw close to his face, blue current pulsed at the claw's tip.

The taller Killborg spoke into a mic built into its shoulder. "This is XB 466 to Commander. We've got him."

What used to be Mike Halloran started moving toward Roger Barris, intent on saving him. Programming and instinct had taken over again. He only made it two steps when a hand reached out of the darkness and pulled him back into cover. "Don't speak," said an unfamiliar voice. It belonged to a stout, shirtless man wearing a red sash and black pants. "They'll hear you," he whispered.

"What?" The stranger's features ran through the scanners and the words "HUMAN MALE - 26 years of age" appeared in the field of view. The system highlighted the barcode tattooed above the man's wrist but couldn't read it.

"My name is Number 1 Man," he said. "The only way we'll get out of this alive is if we work together." His tone was clear. He was someone worth listening to.

Engine noise from above drove them both deeper into cover. A hoverbike from the higher levels sank into the alley, and a girl in a black jumpsuit stepped off. She had a Killborg Insignia on her armband and a bored expression on her face. This girl, no more than twenty years old, was Shadow-Mega.

She wore no armor. She didn't need it.

Killborg XB 466 was preparing to stick Barris with a broad needle but stopped as Shadow-Mega approached. "Commander," he said. "This is the one we've been after. He owes two liters."

She motioned to the Killborgs, and they threw Barris to the ground. He tried to compose himself as he spoke to Shadow-Mega.

"Looks like you're in charge," he said through a split lip. "I was just telling these guys ... lost my calendar -"

Uninterested, Shadow-Mega reached for the man's throat. When her hand grabbed hold, it twisted and shook into a new form. The monstrous claw wrapped around Barris' face, muffling his screams as she dragged him behind a doorway. From the darkness, his screams became clear, along with wet, tearing sounds.

Programming and instinct drove harder than before. What was once Mike Halloran stepped out and yelled at the Killborgs. "NO!"

Number 1 Man stayed hidden but watched closely as the Killborgs looked down the alley.

"What is that?" asked the little one.

"Not one of ours," said XB 466. He shouted, "You! Stay there!"

"... NOPE." Instinct and programming now indicated fleeing. The legs were still awkward, which made fleeing difficult.

"Let's take him out," said XB 466. All three Killborgs jumped, and hover-boards popped under their feet, levitating them. They shot down the alley, closing the distance in an instant.

The little one got clothes-lined by Number 1 Man's arm. The other two paid him no mind as they drew their nightsticks, intent on stopping the strange, augmented man.

The augmented man froze as they approached. His servos and motors clicked on and off as his weapon systems tried to activate. The readout scrolled past his field of view:

PULSE CANNON *** offline *** calibrating*

SONIC GRENADE *** offline *** calibrating*

The nightsticks struck again and again. Pain broke through and he fell to the ground.

FLASH MISSILE *** offline *** calibrating*

PLASMA BEAM *** offline *** calibrating*

The smaller Killborg quickly recovered from Number 1 Man's attack and came at him with fists swinging. Number 1 Man predicted every strike, countered each blow. When he got an opening, he rolled out a *bowstring kick* that sent the Killborg flying.

Number 1 Man felt a presence behind him but turned too late. The hoverbot had approached silently and the stun bolt had already been fired. The intense voltage was impossible to fight; Number 1 Man fell unconscious.

Nearby, focusing on the augmented man's head, the other Killborgs kept swinging their nightsticks.

RAIL PISTOL *** offline *** calibrating*

CHEMICAL NET *** offline *** calibrating*

He was fading out as the pain increased.

BLADE ** *ONLINE* ** *ENGAGED*

XB 466 raised his nightstick for the final strike. He didn't see his target's right gauntlet glow. He didn't hear the pump of the pneumatic system as a long silver blade emerged from the forearm.

The blade went through the Killborg's chin and out the top of his head. With a twist and snap, the blade came free and XB 466's skull split in two. Sparks and blood scattered from the screaming mess of wire and bone. He fell dead.

The two remaining Killborgs beat the strange man down, staying clear of his blade. His readouts were a mess. He could no longer move. The human eye fluttered and just before everything went dark, he saw Shadow-Mega standing above him.

She looked more human than he did. She kicked him, then wiped Roger Barris' blood from her mouth.

———

Pushing her hoverbike well past its maximum speed, Shadow-Mega escorted a Killborg transport through the "HELL USE ONLY" lanes. Meganet City flew past them as their destination grew on the horizon.

All of Hell's lanes led to the Genesis Tower.

The transport was fully loaded with the Blood Crew's collections. On the floor of the cargo area, surrounded by sloshing cannisters and four Killborg guards, a pair of prisoners sat shackled. The one with the red sash and black pants was well known. The one sporting the tech gear was new.

The vehicles passed through the main checkpoint and into the core of Meganet City, where animating billboards greeted the new arrivals with words forty meters high:

Welcome to Meganet City, your new HELL.

Join the fun! Volunteer for experimentation today!

All renegades will be terminated.

Number 1 Man kept watch over his odd accomplice. He saw the human eye begin to open as the other one started to glow. He hoped that was a good sign. They would be arriving soon.

The walls at the base of the Genesis Tower opened, revealing one of its massive hangars. Flags with the Killborg Insignia hung from the high ceilings. Killborg Guards mounted on cruel Hellsteeds rode alongside as Shadow-Mega led the transport to its bay.

Inside the transport, two of the guards started prepping the cannisters for delivery. The Killborg with the metal shoulder kicked the prisoners. "All right, on your feet!" No assistance was offered, so Number 1 Man helped the other captive up.

"Did you read them the thing?" asked the Killborg in charge.

"…maybe?" He was punched in his metal shoulder.

"Do it," said the Killborg in charge. "It's required now, you've got to read them the thing."

"All right, don't hit me." He pressed a button on the back of his glove and some text glowed over his hand. With one breath, he said:

"Welcome to the Genesis Tower Complex. I am bound to remind you that your life is not your own. Hellborn entities rule you and, at their pleasure, may send, fetch, or carry you or yours, be it either body, soul, flesh, blood, or goods, into any place or action of their choosing, be it wheresoever."

"No," said Number 1 Man. "I do not recognize your authority."

"Shut up."

The transport's rear doors opened, and the guards forced the prisoners out. Shadow-Mega stood waiting, just behind The Baron.

"What have you brought for me today?" he asked.

The Killborg in charge grabbed a head in each hand and forced the detainees to look at The Baron. He recognized one of them instantly.

"Ah, welcome back Number 1 Man," said The Baron. "I see your epic escape was short-lived!"

"You're the one who's going to be short-lived!" Number 1 Man struggled against his bonds.

"Yes. You will be greatly rewarded for your … outbursts." The Baron gestured to his eye implants.

"I look forward to it."

"This other one killed XB 466!" said the Killborg in charge.

The Baron walked a circle around the augmented man, trying to understand what he might be.

"Good," he said. "A real fighter. We need more like him." Then he pulled the Killborg in charge close, so no one could hear.

"Did you read them the thing?"

"Yes sir."

The Baron released the Killborg and spun to Shadow-Mega. "Put them with the others, this is excellent work!" Laughing, he lit a cigarette and walked away.

Shadow-Mega stifled a yawn as she tilted her head toward the incarceration ward. Two Killborgs hustled the prisoners through the doors as she strode behind them.

5 / TO THE DEATH, PLEASE

The incarceration ward sat in the bowels of the Genesis Tower Complex. It was a vast open room, like a warehouse. The "cells" weren't individual chambers of concrete and iron bars. They were small, exposed spaces separated by grids of deadly lasers.

The grids were reconfigured often. Cells would grow or shrink depending on the ward's population. Currently, each guest was provided a two-meter square with a bench for resting.

Once she handed off the new arrivals at the processing center, Shadow-Mega spent the next few hours wandering the ward. She found the task dull and pointless, but The Baron insisted on these patrols, so she did them. Today's only bright spot came when Prisoner 237 panicked at the sight of her and ran right into the grid. He was vaporized.

A hoverbot approached with a report. "The new prisoners have been processed and sanitized," it said. "Their number identifications are 8 and 10. They are housed in Row 63." Shadow-Mega nodded and the hoverbot floated off.

She thought that was the end of her duties in the ward. But when the meter-tall hologram of Doctor Scorpius' head popped into existence behind her, she knew there would be more tasks coming. Her eye roll was audible as she turned toward him.

"There you are!" said the Doctor's head. "Urgent directives …

you must ready the arena. And begin data-processing on the new subject immediately!" Shadow-Mega gave a small nod. "The Baron demands more blood. I will be down shortly for my final analysis. Make everything ready. Transmission ends."

She walked through the Doctor's head before it finished fading away. She needed at least fifteen Killborgs to satisfy these new orders, and that meant she'd have to get to the barracks to gather them. On the way, she passed the cells holding Number 1 Man and his mechanical cohort. She ignored them entirely.

———

Prisoner Number 10 sat on a bench behind rows of energy beams. His head hung down with his human eye closed. The lights on his main panel blinked in a nominal pattern, indicating wellness. But in his mind, scenes flashed across his field of view.

Demon teeth ripping skin.

A soldier struggling, blood getting drained.

Count Draculon licking his lips.

He sat upright. A dream? A memory? A glitch? No way to know.

The stark lighting in the cell allowed him to get a good look at himself for the first time. His left hand was still human, for the most part, but from the wrist up it was all machinery.

His entire right arm was mechanical and bulky. From his fingertips to his shoulder, it was a collection of metal and plastic parts.

His chest and legs were a jumble of components, cabling, and lights.

There was no mirror, so he used his human hand to feel his face. He touched skin, and for a moment he was hopeful, but the hope faded as his fingers reached the plating, mesh, and wires that made up most of his head.

He used to be something else, something different. What happened?

A voice from the next cell broke his concentration. "Oy!" it said.

Servos whined as he turned to face his neighbor. His scanners triggered, and "HUMAN MALE - 22 years of age" hovered in his view for a moment. Blond hair in a mullet with a long, thin braid hanging in the back. The sleeveless denim jacket hung open over his bare chest. Scans highlighted the strip of leather cord tied around his bicep and concluded it served no purpose.

The geared, metal gloves on the human male's hands also highlighted. The scan read "FOLDAWAY PULSE PISTOLS ** *disabled*."

"You got a hearing problem, mate?" he said. His accent was Australian. "You answer me when I'm talking to you!"

Across the walkway, Number 1 Man spoke from his cell. "Be still, Justice. Save your energy for the arena."

"Whatever, man," said Justice. "What do you care?"

"What's that supposed to mean?"

Justice scrunched up his face. "What's that supposed to mean?" he said in a tiny voice.

"Stop it!" said Number 1 Man.

"You left us in here to rot," said Justice. "What happened to sticking together?" Shame crept across Number 1 Man's face. "Huh? Can't hear you … seems like nobody's got answers today."

"I had no other choice," said Number 1 Man.

"Yeah, yeah," said Justice. He dismissed Number 1 Man and returned to interrogating his new neighbor. "So, you got a name, buddy?"

Processor lights flashed on and off. What once was Mike Halloran had no memory of his name. He looked at his left hand, the human hand.

"I am …. *man* …"

Then he saw the mechanisms serving as his right hand. "… BORG."

The processing was complete. He had locked his identity. With a whir of motors, he turned to Justice and stated: "My name is: *Manborg*."

"Manborg?" said Justice.

"Uh-huh."

"More like, 'Asshole!'" He snapped into a fighting stance.

"Why don't you just chill out, okay?" Another new voice. This time, it came from the cell next to Number 1 Man's, across the walkway. Manborg's readout displayed "HUMAN FEMALE - 21 years of age."

She had blue hair in a pixie cut, and earrings with light blue leaves. She had painted two red stripes on each cheek and one under her chin. "I can't catch a break around here," she said.

Justice ignored her suggestion to chill out. "Mina, stay out of this." He continued questioning Manborg. "What the hell are you doing here, anyway?" he asked.

Mina's gaze shifted around the ward, trying not to see Justice, Number 1 Man, or Manborg. They were all pissing her off. She turned sideways on her bench and looked down the walkway, rather than engaging with any of them.

"He killed one of theirs." said Number 1 Man. "I trust him. He can help us."

"Us?" said Mina, still looking away. "Now you care about 'us?'"

Shame, again. "Mina, I'm sorry I wasn't here for you."

"Yeah," said Mina. "That's not enough."

Manborg continued scanning Mina. There were defensive gauntlets on each forearm.

"Oy! Man-dork!" said Justice. "What are you staring at?"

His anger was difficult for Manborg to parse.

"You look at my sister like that again," said Justice, "and I'll kill you!"

"Sister?" said Manborg, trying to understand. "She does not speak like you."

"Yeah," said Mina. "He didn't used to talk like that."

"We have accepted it," said Number 1 Man.

"Crikey," said Justice. "Is everyone a drongo?"

The Killborg Insignia on the east wall divided as the doors opened. Doctor Scorpius stepped through.

He was flanked by a hoverbot keeping track of his notes. He

moved through the ward, dragging a leg behind his crutch and snapping orders to the hoverbot.

"Great," said Mina. "Things just keep getting better."

The hoverbot's screen scrolled a list of prisoners and their fighting stats. Doctor Scorpius looked at the occupant of each cell and called out the ones he wanted for the arena.

"Number 3, yes. Not number 4, but we'll take Number 5." He glanced at Mina. "Number 7, yes, she's got speed. With the ones from the other section, how many is that?"

Six, Doctor," said the hoverbot.

"We need three more, then," said Doctor Scorpius. He found a surprise in the cell next to Mina's. "Ah, Number 1 Man, you've returned. Your new number is 8, and you're going in."

Manborg's cell was next. Doctor Scorpius scrutinized him. "So," he said, "you are the new arrival. You look unique, Number 10." He turned to the hoverbot. "We'll take him. Let's see what he can do."

The Doctor resumed limping through his rounds. "Number 9, Justice, you're in as well."

"Traitor," said Justice.

Doctor Scorpius kept moving. He didn't look back as he said, "Fight hard today. You might get out of this alive." Turning toward the next row of cells, deeper in the ward, he encountered The Baron, along with a security hoverbot.

"Have the prisoners been processed? Ready for combat?" asked The Baron.

"Of course," said Doctor Scorpius.

"Do not fail us, Doctor." The Baron gave him a light slap on the cheek, and as he stepped away, he kicked the Doctor's crutch and Scorpius dropped to the floor.

The Baron continued down Row 63 with his hoverbot close behind. "I shall take great pleasure in watching their bodies, bloodied and broken, scattered across the …" He paused in front of Mina's cell. "Oh, hello! Who's this?"

"Prisoner Number 7, sir," said the hoverbot.

"Such a beautiful name," sighed The Baron.

"That's not my name," said Mina.

"Yes. The perfect specimen," said The Baron. "Forgive me, Prisoner Number 7, where are my manners? Are you comfortable? Can I get you anything?"

"You can get lost."

The Baron's face contorted into a jagged smile. "Such a firebrand!" The hoverbot's screen began to flash.

"You are requested in the control room, sir," it said.

"What?" said The Baron. "Oh, all right. Sorry, Prisoner Number 7. As you can see, I have to do *everything* around here. Perhaps when all your friends are destroyed, we can find a little more time to chat. I've got my own nightmare chamber ... enticing, eh?"

"I'd rather be dead," said Mina.

"Indeed! We have so much in common. Be seeing you!" With that, The Baron walked away with a little more spring in his step than when he arrived.

Lights flashed and a low siren howled. The lasers in front of the chosen prisoners' cells withdrew into the ceiling. Without prompting, the prisoners lined up in the walkway as Killborg guards took their places around them. The one with the largest gun said, "Get moving, all of you."

Manborg took his place in the line and walked with the rest. Justice was glad to be out and did some fancy stepping as he moved along. One of the guards gave him a jolt with a buzzstick. "No dancing," he said.

"Hey!" said Justice, rubbing his arm. "... fuck."

———

The Terroropticon, an enormous arena resting in the shadow of the Genesis Tower, was home to at least three matches a day. The fear, anger, and occasional hope that coursed through the veins of the fighters made theirs the most valued blood on Earth. The floor of the combat field was an astringent construct, designed to pull in and capture every drop spilled there.

The stands held 140,000 Hellborn fans, ready to watch terrible monsters or squads of Killborgs battling human warriors. They shouted for their favorites and chugged down cut-rate plasma on draft.

A few of the human fighters had admirers as well. Somebody always roots for the underdog, even in Hell.

That's why the stadium went wild when Number 1 Man entered the arena. He was famous, and everyone had heard about his escape. He had betrayed his fans and angered his haters even more.

His face on the 30-meter screens in the Terroropticon was the first news of his recapture.

He was back, and the crowd wanted blood.

In his lab, Doctor Scorpius had all the contenders and their stats broken down across every monitor, along with live feeds from the arena. He paid particular attention to Prisoner Number 10.

The address system crackled, and an electronic voice echoed over the stadium. "Battle will commence in one minute. T minus, 60 seconds." A countdown clock appeared on all the giant screens and the stands shook with cheering.

From the center of the arena's field, Justice looked out at the crowd. He had painted black stripes on his face to match his sister's. "Freaks," he said. "Blood drinking freaks, all of them." He grabbed Manborg by the shoulder. "You get in my way, and I'll kill ya."

Manborg couldn't isolate Justice's voice from the crowd noise. "What?" he said. Justice flexed his muscles in response.

Pulling off her warmup jacket, Mina eyed the two massive doors on the far side of the arena. Number 1 Man approached and said, "Mina, be careful. I've got your back." She ignored him.

The countdown concluded, and a hologram of The Baron's head, twice the size of the largest screens, appeared hovering over the field. No matter where you sat, he was looking at you. "Welcome," he said, "to the Terroropticon. Hello human combatants! There are no losers here. You either win, or you die ... but now that I say it out loud, that sounds a lot like losing. Well, let the games begin!"

The great doors rolled open and the crowd got even louder. Two convoys of armor-clad Killborgs roared in on hoverbikes. They moved in a circle, surrounding the humans, forcing them into the center of the field.

Three days ago, Melody Baker got arrested for a curfew violation. Now, she stood in the arena. If she survived, they'd let her go home.

She'd been given a machete and a helmet. She didn't know what to do.

As one of the hoverbikes passed her, the rider used a kickblade to cut her in half. She died in the first six seconds of the match.

As soon as her body fell, the arena floor reacted, pulling in blood. All around her the ground turned red. Moments later, the crimson color faded as her plasma wicked into the collection vats below and she was left a desiccated husk.

Mina, Number 1 Man, Justice, and Manborg stood together, back-to-back in defense positions. "Bikers. They're not fooling around," said Justice.

"I want to help," said Manborg.

"Just stay clear," said Justice.

"We need him or we're all dead!" said Number 1 Man.

"Yeah? And how would you know?"

Mina saw the bikers closing in. "Hey! Can everybody shut up? It's time to focus, bro."

For a moment, Manborg watched the arena fade away.

It was replaced by a city.

A familiar face spoke to him.

Then his mind jumped back to reality. "Don't call me 'Bro,'" said Manborg

"I am certain she was talking to Justice," said Number 1 Man.

"And she's right," said Justice. "Less yacking, more attacking." He tried to give Manborg a high-five, but Manborg didn't know what to do with it.

Mina pulled two thin blades from behind her back. "Just watch me." She ran at the oncoming hoverbikes.

"Mina, no!" said Number 1 Man.

Mina skipped for three steps to set up, then made a broad leap. She landed straddling the handlebars of a passing bike. "Get off!" said the Killborg rider.

She gave him a smile, then used the blades as two-handed shears and sliced his head off. Before the bike went into the wall, she rolled off and landed running. She was on the hunt for her next target.

The screens flashed Mina's promo photo, the one with her holding a handful of knives and winking. A group of Killborgs in the cheap seats had blue wigs and red stripes painted on their faces. They cheered like mad.

"Game on!" said Justice. Manborg's readout indicated the pulse pistols were *active*.

Justice stretched his arms, and that made silver guns twist out of his metal gloves. They snapped into place as he planted his feet and took careful aim at one of the circling bikes. He fired, and the pulse bolt blew the Killborg's hands to bits.

The Killborg shrieked, trying to steer with bloody stumps. The hoverbike veered hard and Justice had to jump out of the way. He got clear just before the bike flipped and exploded.

The screens all read "KILL," and the crowd became more agitated.

A Killborg foot soldier with a long flail and heavy helmet was marching toward Mina. She spun her blades and steadied herself. Number 1 Man stepped in front of her and drew the attacker's attention.

"To the death, please," said Number 1 Man.

The flail swung wildly as the Killborg charged. Number 1 Man timed a *whirlwind kick* that knocked the weapon to one side. With his opponent off-balance, Number 1 Man made a *shock punch* to the throat followed by a *skyward pine* uppercut to the base of the helmet.

The helmet was so heavy that the force of the blow bent the Killborg's head backwards, tearing his neck open, nearly decapitating him.

Justice was doing the same fancy stepping he tried earlier, but this time his moves were punctuated by pistol shots. Killborgs fell right and left. He even managed to hit a few of the freaks catcalling him from the stands.

The knives kept flying from Mina's fingertips. She noticed Manborg, looking everywhere, trying to evaluate what was happening. "You gonna help any time soon?" she asked.

"Yeah," said Justice, firing. "Less brooding, more shooting!"

Before Manborg could respond, a Killborg twice his size came out of nowhere and swung a huge tomahawk at his head. In that moment, Mina thought she'd see Manborg die.

But programming and instinct took over. Manborg grabbed the Killborg's wrist before the tomahawk made contact. The Killborg used its other hand to deal a series of savage punches to Manborg's stomach.

His armor blocked those easily as new readouts appeared.

"BRACE ** PREPARE FOR RECOIL."

Manborg pushed the Killborg back two meters and felt his legs clamp down.

PULSE CANNON ** *ONLINE* ** *ENGAGED*

His right hand lit up and changed. Components rolled out and locked in place. His forearm was bigger than his torso now, and it was all one weapon. Mina stared as he swung the barrel around to the Killborg and unleashed a storm of pulse bolts that tore the creature to shreds.

Manborg looked towards Mina for approval. The weapon kept firing. He didn't know how to make it stop.

Mina dodged to safety as the gun propelled Manborg in a tight circle, eliminating four more bikers on the field and six of Hell's denizens in the stands. He fell onto his back, shooting in the air.

Above all that chaos, Mina heard laughter. The last hoverbike was making a tight turn, aiming the spiked front-end right at her.

The laughter came from the rider. A pained, insane laugh. One of Manborg's stray pulse bolts had taken off a piece of the Killborg's head.

It didn't have long to live. And it wasn't going to go alone.

Justice fired again and again, but he kept missing the target.

Mina reached back, and found she was out of knives. Instead, she readied her fists.

From across the arena, Number 1 Man ran at a full sprint. He leapt into a *gull over the water* kick that knocked the Killborg off the bike and crushed his chest as they landed.

The crowd went silent as the bike slowed to a stop, then tipped over.

There were no enemies left on the field. The only humans left were Mina, Justice, Number 1 Man, and Manborg.

On his back, Manborg continued struggling. The weapon had stopped firing, but it was still extended. He was off-balance, unable to stand. "I'm sorry. I'm sorry," he kept repeating.

Mina and Number 1 Man couldn't bear to look at him like that. Justice never noticed; he was too busy taunting the crowd. "Hey, you bloody freaks! Rack off!"

The screens flashed a new message: "HUMANS WIN."

The crowd hissed and demanded blood as the victors were escorted off the field. Manborg stumbled along last.

Up in the cheap seats, the Killborgs in the blue wigs were pummeling everyone around them. They really loved that girl …

———

Doctor Scorpius had been watching Manborg, and he was concerned. He zoomed into a replay and watched frame-by-frame as the pulse canon extended. His study was interrupted as the screen began to flicker.

All the screens flashed. Doctor Scorpius felt his fear grow as he realized what was coming. The monitors formed a patchwork of images that combined into a single subject: a pair of dark, deep-set eyes.

Then he heard the voice of Count Draculon.

"Doctor …"

A low droning sound pulsed in every corner of the lab. It cut through the Doctor's head. The meters on his wrist interface spiked. "Why!?" he cried. "What have I done!?"

"You promised these games would bring blood," said The Count.

"They're working together ... this isn't the first time they've won ..." He tried to adjust his pain actuators, but it only made things worse.

The words came from all around now, instead of just from the screens. "There is no more room for mistakes," said Draculon. "Not again."

The sound and images stopped. The screens returned to their normal feeds, and Doctor Scorpius buckled. "Yes," he said.

"Yes, Master."

A STATIC-LADEN VOICE CRACKLED OUT OF THE SPEAKER ON THE WALL. "Step on the plate and face the health station," it said.

Justice hopped on, lined up his feet with the outlines on the plate and faced the tall, cylindrical machine. He flinched when he got a close look at the unit. Its components were in working order, but there were splashes of dried blood, patches of grease, and less specific stains all over it.

"This thing's festy," he said.

He was right. In fact, everything in the room was old and sticky. They were in a sealed holding area, the last stop before they returned to their cells in the incarceration ward. Mina and Number 1 Man had already been through the health station. They sat on the other side of the room. Manborg stood behind Justice, waiting his turn.

Rods emerged from the unit, glowing blue. They moved up, down, and around Justice, then paused.

"Raise your arms."

He did so, and the rods did another pass then retracted. After some noisy clicking, the voice announced: "Subject cleared to return to cell. No internal injuries, no broken bones. Minor cuts and scrapes detected, please use this topical solution towelette." A bell rang, a slot opened, and the unit dispensed a faded packet with a moistened healing pad inside.

"Step down."

Justice took the packet and threw it at the machine. It bounced hard then landed on the floor.

Mina picked it up, saying. "I save these, you know." She already had one laying across a raw patch on her arm.

"I understand your frustration, Justice," said Number 1 Man. "The true purpose of this devise is making certain we did not smuggle anything out of the arena."

"Deadset," said Justice. He watched the machine shut down and roll into a cubby. "Hey! You prodded all of us, but you didn't check Manborg!" He punched the wall as it closed around the health station. "What about him?"

"It only works on people," said Mina.

"Ah!" said Justice. He got in Manborg's face. "You know, those were some pretty fancy schenanigrams you pulled out there. What the hell are you anyway?"

"Are you a spy?" asked Number 1 Man. "Did Doctor Scorpius send you?"

"That health gizmo doesn't think you're human," said Mina. "Are you here to kill us?"

Manborg did his best to craft a response. "I came here -"

Justice put a finger to Manborg's lips. "Don't answer that, you dickhead!" He pulled his hand away, then turned his back.

"He almost got Mina killed! I saw it," said Number 1 Man.

"Son-of-a-bitch," said Justice, He continued his turn and got in Manborg's face again. "You almost got my sister killed! I can't believe this!"

"What kind of a man would do such a thing?" asked Number 1 Man.

"He's not a man," said Mina. "He's one of them."

"You're right Mina. He probably is."

Justice stepped away and punched the air. "Shit!"

"I am ... not one of them," said Manborg. "I am ... something else."

An announcement came over the speaker. "Please stand by. Guards have been dispatched to escort you to the ward."

"We didn't survive this long," said Justice, "so you could dance in here in your shiny boots and electro-schenanigram outfits and get us all killed!" Number 1 Man held Justice in place, preventing a fight.

Manborg felt regret. He wished he'd been more useful in the arena. Justice kept shouting. "Get out! You heard me!"

He scanned the perimeter of the holding area, and the ceiling and floor, but Manborg found no exits.

"Take a hike," said Justice. "Get out!" Manborg walked a few steps. When he reached the wall. He turned back to Justice, hoping for clearer instructions.

"Yeah," said Justice. "Stick out your thumb, hitch a ride, and go. Because you're not wanted here."

Manborg tried to follow the command, but his maneuver resulted in an awkward thumbs-up. The rest of the group stared at him.

Silent. Angry.

He faced the wall, hung his head, and waited for the guards.

Number 1 Man put his hand on Mina's shoulder. "It's ok, you're safe now."

————

"Oh! Hello there, Prisoner Number 7!" said The Baron. Mina had been back in her cell for less than an hour. She was still dabbing her arm, trying to get the last drops of liquid out of the healing pad when The Baron came by.

She knew he was coming. She heard him whistling a tune as he walked to her cell. Her eyes stayed locked on her arm as he stood on the other side of the laser grid, trying to make conversation.

"I ... I hope I'm not interrupting," said The Baron.

Nothing.

He tried again. "So! Do you like hoverbikes?"

Nothing.

"Or …"

Her eyes shifted to him. They carried disdain.

Defeated, he turned and spoke to himself. "Shit … Baron, you are so stupid!" He still had a chance to make a decent exit. He gave Mina a big wave.

"Well, I'm on my way. Good luck!" He stepped back from her cell and into the laser barrier on the other side of the walkway. It shocked him, but there was no damage.

"Gah! Woah … where did those beams come from? There should be a sign or something. Okay, bye now." He hurried away, talking to himself again.

"Such an idiot … idiot!" He passed a hoverbot on his way out and loudly proclaimed, "I'll be in my nightmare chamber!"

The hoverbot continued down Row 63 and stopped in front of Manborg's cell. "Get up," it said as the laser grid receded.

None of the other cells opened. Whatever was happening next was for Manborg alone.

He rose and followed the hoverbot toward the doors. On the way, he looked carefully at the others. If he never returned here, he wanted to remember these people.

He dropped something on the way out. The hoverbot didn't spot it.

There was a long silence after Manborg went through the doors. Number 1 Man finally spoke. "I don't think he's coming back."

Mina saw the scrap that Manborg left in the walkway. She reached slowly between the beams and picked it up.

It was a photograph of two men in happier times. She felt like she knew one of them, somehow. She covered half of the younger one's face with her thumb and saw Manborg.

———

The Genesis Tower had an observation deck overlooking the Terroropticon. All the controls for the arena and stadium operations were there, opposite a glass wall with a stunning view of the venue.

Using a holographic touch interface, Doctor Scorpius was making final entries for the next match. The stadium was full, the fighters were in their staging areas. If the countdown didn't start soon, that crowd might start causing trouble.

But the work kept getting interrupted as The Baron paced around the room.

"What can I be doing wrong?" he said. "I mean, I'm trying so hard."

The Doctor tried to split his focus between his work and his boss. "Yes. I see."

"I … how can I know how she feels?" The Baron moved nearer, became harder to ignore. "You can process human emotions, so what do you think? Because sometimes I feel like she doesn't even know I exist."

The Doctor made an error and had to start a command string over again. "Um, I don't know, have you tried … buying her something? Bringing her something? Flowers, maybe?"

"Silence! Stop right there."

The error was corrected quickly. Did The Baron see it?

"Yes?" said Doctor Scorpius.

"What kind of flowers? Will she like a certain kind? I don't want to get it wrong."

This conversation was never going to end, but it had to end if the match was ever going to begin. The Doctor had to risk upsetting The Baron. "You'll have to forgive me Baron, but I'm terribly busy here. You've given me a lot of work to do. Perhaps you can discuss this with, I don't know, the Count? You two seem to get along well. Very well."

"Uh, yeah … when he's sober." The Baron returned to pacing. "I feel a freaking anxiety attack coming on. I've got to sit down." He moved to a bench by the window and lit a cigarette.

"You told me you quit," said Doctor Scorpius.

"Don't start," said The Baron. "And get that countdown going, will you? The match is running late."

————

At last, the massive screens around the arena lit up with animated fire and the words "ARE YOU READY?" Every creature stood and hollered as the 60 second countdown began.

In the center of the field, looking tiny, Manborg stood alone. The crowd chanted for his death. He stared at the doors, knowing his opponents were on the other side. Nothing in his scans or readouts gave him any information about what those opponents might be.

Music started. The fans stomped and clapped along. The screens flashed a message:

He is coming!

And the crowd cheered.

Let him hear your RAGE!

And the crowd roared. In slow motion, timed to the music, video ran with a monster tearing people apart. The weapons mounted to the beast's shoulders liquified groups of humans attempting to flee.

Another message burst on the screens as the doors slowly opened.

2,073 confirmed kills!

He is …

THE CHAMPION!!!

The Terroropticon shook as everyone watching went into a frenzy. It got even louder, more out of control as the creature lumbered into the arena.

It had to duck. It was much taller than the opening.

"The Champion" earned that name because the beast never lost a fight. Years ago, it had another name: Shadow-Grandis. This was the first prototype created for the Shadow Project. Doctor Scorpius lost control of the mutation process, and this was the result. A four-meter-tall creature with bony growths tearing through its thick hide. There was no way to control it, no capacity for reason.

So, they implanted weapons and the beast was given free rein in the arena. At all other times, it was heavily sedated.

The Champion ignored Manborg and stood to its full height, racking its shoulder-mounted guns and brandishing the huge, spiked mace that stood in for its left hand. The stadium erupted. The monster found the screams pleasurable.

Holographic projections with a live feed of the match ran in every row of the incarceration ward. Justice punched the air. "No one should have to go up against The Champion alone!" Mina and Number 1 Man agreed.

This was wrong.

In the arena, Manborg stepped toward his opponent, but misjudged the creature's reach. It swept the mace-hand and launched Manborg to the other side of the field. Even in the cheap seats, they heard the impact when he landed.

He stood after the second bounce. His inertial dampeners locked in and prevented any damage. But as soon as he was upright, The Champion fired the arc guns on its shoulders, sending a fierce ball of lightning across the arena and tossing Manborg again.

All the prisoners in the ward were glued to the match now.

"This is terrible," said Number 1 Man.

"I can't watch this," said Justice, watching intently.

Mina couldn't look away. She was hanging on to hope.

The Champion moved slowly, but it only took four steps for it to cross the arena and grab Manborg in its huge, mutated fist. It shook him hard, like it wanted to hear his insides rattle.

The fist was crushing Manborg's chest. His readout showed:

WARNING ** *pressure danger*

As he bounced around, Manborg kept staring into the creature's lidless eyes. Targeting systems took over.

PLASMA BEAM ** *ONLINE ** ENGAGED*

An insulated tube snaked out of his head and fired an intense beam of energy into the creature's eyeball. The Champion dropped Manborg and backed away, rocking its enormous head back and forth in pain.

In the ward, Mina's hope was growing.

The crowd in the Terroropticon catcalled and hissed. They were expecting a kill and got ripped off. The boos turned to cheers, however, as The Champion shook off the pain and turned to Manborg.

Manborg hadn't moved from where he was dropped. He was on his hands and knees, trying to regroup. As the crowd cheered, he rose and faced The Champion.

"No way," he said, and shook his wrist. "Eat pulse cannon."

PULSE CANNON ** *offline* ** *cooldown*

"Oh," said Manborg. The Champion was getting closer. Manborg raised his hand to his eyepiece, trying to find the fault in the cannon. This bent-arm position exposed a launch tube in his elbow, which started beeping.

FLASH MISSILE ** ONLINE ** ENGAGED

"Okay," said Manborg

CHOOSE TARGETING MODE: *Manual or Automatic?*

"Automatic. Go! Kill that!" said Manborg.

He watched as a reticle locked onto The Champion's head. Manborg felt his legs brace, and his arm fired a missile into the monster's face. It struck with a bright flash followed by a torrent of flames and smoke.

The incarceration ward was cheering.

Mina nodded her head, smiling.

Justice danced in his cell.

"Yummy," said Number 1 Man.

When the flames and smoke cleared, The Champion had a pulpy, red and black hole where its head and clavicles used to be. The remaining bulk collapsed, lifeless.

Even in the cheap seats, they heard the impact when it landed.

For the second time today, the screens read "HUMANS WIN."

———

A hoverbot's scanning beam crept over every centimeter of Manborg's cell. Shadow-Mega supervised the process from the Row 63 walkway. The Baron paced nearby, puffing frantically on a Percheron Black.

"No one has ever won against The Champion," said The Baron. "How did this happen?!"

Number 1 Man spoke from his cell. "I guess there's a new champion in town."

"Don't think I've forgotten about you," said The Baron.

"How could you? I ripped out both your eyes."

Sputtering, The Baron turned away.

The hoverbot shut down the beam. "Scan complete. Nothing found," it said. Shadow-Mega gave a hand signal to the hoverbot and it floated off. She turned to The Baron with a sigh and awaited instructions.

He tossed his cigarette onto the floor and ground it with this boot. "I want that man ... borg ... whatever he is! I want him brought to the lab. Make sure he's restrained. Get him there! It's time we found out what he is."

———

His duel with The Champion left Manborg weak. He was almost glad when the Killborgs and hoverbots escorted him from the Terroropticon. The crowd wanted to destroy him, and he didn't have the strength to fight 140,000 angry fans.

This time, they didn't take him to the holding area. They took him to a lab, laden with equipment. His scans failed to identify any of it, but he recognized Shadow-Mega.

She stood by an operating table in the center of the room. It powered up and rotated to a vertical position. The guard detail held Manborg's back against the table as the hoverbots interfaced with the controls. Energy beams and metal straps worked in concert, binding his legs, waist, wrists, and neck.

The hoverbots drifted off as The Baron entered the lab. He

approached the table slowly, studying. "So, this is Manborg," he said.

There was no response. Manborg held still, eyes front, ignoring his interrogator. The Baron poked at the mesh and wires on Manborg's shoulder. "Fancy," he said. "Shame that you are still just a man. Do you look forward to being pulled apart, piece by piece?"

With a whir of motors, Manborg turned his head and glared at The Baron. "Uh-huh!"

"I saw you protect your human friends in the arena. Would you like to see them beg for their lives?"

"Yeah, great!" Manborg still hadn't blinked.

"Yes … *super*-great," said The Baron. He turned to Shadow-Mega. "Execute the remaining prisoners." She smiled and walked towards the door. The Baron called after her. "Oh, except for Prisoner Number 7."

He didn't see her smile drop as she left for the incarceration ward.

The Baron got close to Manborg's face again, the smell of cigarettes travelled with his words. "Shadow-Mega is one of our finest creations. A hybrid like you. She will show your friends what pain really is."

"Yeah right," said Manborg.

"I know I'm right," said The Baron. "The city will drink their blood. But you … we'll save you for when HE returns."

"Oh really?"

"Yeah, really. The Count has … become something. Something unstoppable. Even you will beg for his mercy." The Baron called over his shoulder. "Doctor Scorpius, find out how this thing works."

Manborg hadn't seen the Doctor come in. Didn't know how long he'd been watching. The Baron stormed out, leaving Manborg and Doctor Scorpius alone.

The Doctor spoke slowly. Deliberately. "Can you hear me?"

"Yes," said Manborg.

"Good … good … my name is Doctor Scorpius. And what is your name?"

"Manborg."

The Doctor focused on Manborg's chest panel, his finger tracing the wires. "I see ... very good. Where are you from?"

"I woke up in a box."

"Then all of this must be very strange to you," said Doctor Scorpius, his mind still wandering. "This isn't the world you were expecting to wake up in, is it?"

"No," said Manborg. "I was -"

"A soldier, yes," said the Doctor, finding his focus. "In the great war against Hell."

That made Manborg blink. "Yes. How did you know that?"

"I know," said Doctor Scorpius, "because I built you."

7 / *GETTING AWAY FROM IT ALL*

The holographic clipboard hovering next to Shadow-Mega diagramed the cell layout in the incarceration ward. She checked and rechecked it against the control panel at the end of Row 63.

Executing all the prisoners, as The Baron ordered, was a simple matter of setting all the laser grids in motion so they crossed each other. An economical way to incinerate every person in every cell. But then he made it complicated. She wasn't supposed to take out *all* the prisoners. One cell would need to remain unchanged, the one with Prisoner Number 7.

Finding the most efficient means to carry out a command was one of Shadow-Mega's prime directives. She was sorting out a solution that only required a single button push.

From her cell, Mina had been watching Shadow-Mega work. "Hey, bud" she said. There was no response.

"Are you in there?" asked Mina. "Did they leave even one memory?"

Again, nothing. Shadow-Mega continued her project. Mina shook her head.

"What the hell did they do to you?"

———

"No! I don't believe you!" said Manborg, fighting his bonds.

"Doesn't matter," said Doctor Scorpius, turning a component on Manborg's chest.

"What are you doing to me?"

"I'm reducing the limiters on your power intakes. You've had enough time for burn in. And I'll ask the questions if you don't mind." He opened a small panel on the side of Manborg's head and toggled three switches. "There, that will enable some of your higher functions." Manborg felt … different. Saw images, pieces of his life. Of his brother.

"I built you when mankind fell," said Doctor Scorpius. "I used their robotic advances, stole their Hell-tech. I adapted the best artillery Hell had to offer. You are a weapon powerful enough to stop them! A hero to save us all."

More images, more memories.

Boners attacking.

Missed shots.

Friends dying.

"I am not a hero," said Manborg.

"You don't know what you are," said Doctor Scorpius. "Your systems are still coming together. Soon, though, you'll be complete. You've only been active for thirty-two hours and you already have them rattled."

"Why did you do this?"

"I had to! This whole nightmare is my doing. I was the one who let them in! For science."

———

In the months leading up to April 8th, 1987, a secret project was underway at the Stanford Linear Accelerator Center (SLAC) in Menlo Park, California.

The internet's TCP/IP protocols had just been introduced, and the limitless sharing of data became a reality. A global workflow for research and the advancement of everyone and everything was possible. It was as if an information eclipse finally ended, and the sunlight of knowledge flooded every lab in the world.

A small group of brilliant minds made a pact to ignore borders. Fearing their governments would punish them for revealing their best sciences, they agreed to never meet in person. To keep their identities private.

Doctor Evan Scorpius became their covert leader. He gathered and distributed the information amongst this cabal of technologists. The newly formed world wide web became their clandestine base of operations.

And they made progress. Doctor Scorpius didn't know where or who his colleagues were, but that didn't matter. They were saving the world.

Fusion.

They were nearing a simple, elegant solution to fusion. A gallon of rainwater to power a city, safely, for a year. Easily held micro-generators would eliminate the concept of scarcity for everyone.

The plans fell into place. This breakthrough was possible with today's equipment. This could happen right now.

Why had this technology been hidden? Did it reside in countries dependent on strength from fossil fuels? Would a solution that leveled the playing field for every soul on the planet make them weak?

For Doctor Scorpius and his colleagues to put the rich and powerful in their place, they needed to create a device for the proof of concept. A working model for the global population to see in action. People would be invited to examine it, any attempt to debunk the technology would be welcomed.

But such attempts would fail and make the message stronger. A message that would be carried on the new internet.

They had the plans, but they needed funding. So, the cabal followed the same path to funding and success they'd seen their governments follow so many times before.

They lied.

They said they were constructing a "large detector" at SLAC.

They would have to close the facility for at least three months to build the thing. With it, they'd knock photons around and observe dark matter behavior and advance our understanding of the cosmos. The rich and powerful got out their checkbooks. Empires salivated over what they would discover and control using this fancy new toy.

The machine came together on schedule. The cabal kept their word to each other, and the real purpose, creating power for all, stayed quiet.

And on April 8th, 1987, at 11:32 am, Doctor Scorpius made a little speech at the facility in Menlo Park and threw the switch.

And discovered he was lied to.

In fact, the cabal itself was a lie.

He hadn't been conspiring with anonymous scientists from totalitarian lands. They were the denizens of Hell. And Doctor Evan Scorpius, ruled by avarice, by his need to rescue the world and be a hero, had become their willing puppet.

The machine didn't create fusion power. It didn't save the world.

It opened the Inferno Gate. And in moments the world was torn apart, but Doctor Scorpius was saved, to witness what he had done.

And now, he continues in Hell's employ.

———

"You," said Manborg. "You caused all of this?"

"Yes. And when I finally realized what was happening, it was far too late. You are my last hope for redemption. But now... it seems that time has run out for us all!"

"You dick," said Manborg. "It's all your fault!" He felt power surging through his circuits, the result of the adjustments Doctor Scorpius made before. The energy beams and metal straps were failing. His rage was stronger than his restraints.

Manborg stepped forward and the operating table blew to pieces around him.

He was free.

Alarms sounded throughout the Genesis Tower. The lighting in the incarceration ward went red. The schematic on Shadow-Mega's clipboard grew larger, with the lab area flashing. There was a breach.

"Sounds like your day just got busier," said Mina.

Shadow-Mega glared at her as she snapped the board shut and sealed the control panel on the wall. Under her jumpsuit, her legs made popping noises as they grew, then she ran out of the ward with inhuman speed.

Walking across the lab, Manborg felt entirely stable on his legs for the first time. He saw fear building in the doctor's eyes as he got closer.

The interface on Doctor Scorpius' wrist featured a small-burst energy tool. He fired it at Manborg, knowing it wouldn't do any good. "Stop! Please stop!" He tripped over his crutch and landed on the floor.

Doctor Scorpius said, "You were a hero. I saw your last moments. You defied Count Draculon himself."

The words triggered more memories.

Firing a rifle.

Dodging a great sword.

Manborg stopped. "Go on," he said.

"I planned it so that you would awaken in the future," said Doctor Scorpius, standing. "Now you have power to match your conviction. You can face Draculon and finish what you started all those years ago!"

"Why is this happening to me?" asked Manborg.

Before he could answer, Doctor Scorpius heard the door beeping. Someone was trying to open the lock. "We're out of time," he said.

Outside the lab, Shadow-Mega's eyes rolled black. She tripled in size as her skin transformed into a thick hide housing bunched, ropey muscles. She raised her enormous fists over her head and brought them down on the door.

"Here, take this," said Doctor Scorpius. He handed Manborg a cassette tape. "It's a future-cassette. All the answers you seek lie within it."

Manborg stored the cassette. "Thanks man."

The pounding got stronger. The door made buckling noises; light came in from its edges. "You can get out through there," said Doctor Scorpius, pointing to a hatchway on the other side of the lab.

The lock-panel next to the hatchway highlighted in Manborg's view. His eyepiece zoomed in on the panel and a string of code flew by, hacking it.

The panel blinked and the hatch opened. Manborg looked back to Doctor Scorpius. "Yes," said the doctor. "You have many skills." Manborg started toward the hatch but felt the doctor touch his shoulder.

"Manborg," said Doctor Scorpius, "I only helped them because there was no other choice."

"I understand," said Manborg.

"Make things right again."

"I WILL!!!" said Manborg. He ran through the hatch, and it sealed behind him.

———

The incarceration ward swam with blaring alarms, pulsing red lights, and shouting prisoners. Mina, Justice, and Number 1 Man focused on each other.

"All the Killborgs ran off," said Mina. "Now is our chance to get out of here."

"But how?" asked Number 1 Man. "We're trapped behind these laser barriers!"

A lone hoverbot tried to maintain order. "Stop talking," it said.

Justice was pacing. "Aw, where's Manborg and his gizmos when you need him?"

"Stop talking."

Without any warning, the large Killborg Insignia on the east wall blew apart. A familiar figure moved through the resulting smoke and dust.

"No way," said Justice.

The figure stepped into the light. It was Manborg, and he was smiling. "Hello everyone."

The hoverbot approached him, charging up its claws. "Stop talking."

"*You* stop talking," said Manborg. A rail pistol extended from his left forearm and fired three bursts, disintegrating the hoverbot.

"I thought that thing would never shut up," said Justice. "Manborg, get us outta here!"

Manborg scanned the area, tracking miles of energy conduit in the ceiling. It all led to a series of control panels on the walls. This system was more complex than the simple lock he hacked upstairs.

"Shoot the control panel to free us from our cells," said Number 1 Man.

"Oh, okay," said Manborg. The plasma beam fired from the tube in his head. Its intense energy destroyed the panel.

That started a chain reaction. The plasma energy fed through the conduits and burned out their connections. Every laser barrier in the incarceration ward flickered out.

It took a few moments for the prison population to realize what had happened. Then they cheered and mobbed the only exit, the gap in the wall that Manborg created when he arrived.

"We're not going that way," said Justice. "Those guys are crackers."

"We can escape through the hangar bay," said Number 1 Man. "It's one level below us if we go through the southern doors."

Mina was on the floor, reaching under her bench. She pulled out a tattered bundle. It was full of blade-paks; dispensers loaded with her weapon of choice. She holstered them under her warmup jacket.

"How did you get those?" asked Justice.

"I saved them."

"We must leave now," said Number 1 Man. With equal measures

of fear and hope, they ran toward the southern exits. But Manborg stayed behind.

Mina stopped after a few steps when she realized Manborg wasn't moving. "You coming with us?" she asked.

"Am I allowed to?"

"Yeah," said Mina. "Just don't shoot me or anything." She handed him the photo. He looked at it, smiled, and stored it away.

"Besides," said Mina, "we need you to blow open the southern door."

Once Manborg blew open the southern door, Number 1 Man led the way. He knew the layout of the Genesis Tower.

They used a maintenance shaft to travel down one level then ran through a series of tunnels, aiming for the hangar bays.

"There will be hover vehicles in the bay," said Number 1 Man. "They are always charged and ready."

The last tunnel fed into a hallway lined with video screens. The alarms were getting louder. Each screen showed a different sector, and in each sector, guards battled rioting prisoners.

"Let's hope that keeps the guards on the upper levels," said Mina.

A low droning sound thrummed in the hall. "What's that noise?" asked Number 1 Man.

The sound built up. "It hurts," said Mina.

"Let's get out of here," said Justice.

All the screens flashed and flickered as the group ran down the hall. Manborg stayed back. Something held him there.

The monitors formed a patchwork of images that combined into a single subject: a pair of dark, deep-set eyes. He heard harsh laughter, saw images in his mind.

Demon teeth ripping skin.

A soldier struggling, blood getting drained.

"Manborg!" called Justice. "Hurry up, get away from those TVs!"

The screens burst outward, showering Manborg with glass and flames. He ran clear of the explosions and joined the others. "What the hell was that?" asked Mina.

"We have to keep moving," said Manborg.

They all gathered in front of a thick security door at the end of the hall. "The hangar is through there," said Number 1 Man.

Mina pulled on the lever. The door's border flashed red, and a speaker crackled. "Access denied."

"Shit," said Mina. "It's got a future-lock."

There was a heavy thud behind them. Shadow-Mega had dropped through a grate in the ceiling. She was only twenty meters away.

Manborg stepped between Shadow-Mega and the others and fired his pulse cannon. Every bolt struck her, but it wasn't causing any damage. He was slowing her down, but she kept getting closer.

"Justice," said Number 1 Man, "are your pistols working? You can shoot the lock."

Justice snapped his wrists and his guns spun out. "Oh yes!"

He fired seven rounds in rapid succession before the lock burst. Then the door rolled up.

"Everybody, get in there!" said Justice. The group moved through, but Manborg held his ground, trying to keep Shadow-Mega from advancing. Mina grabbed him. "We have to go," she said.

Manborg stopped firing and moved with Mina. She looked back and locked eyes with Shadow-Mega as the door dropped and sealed, putting an obstacle between them.

"Let's go," said Mina, and everyone moved into the hangar.

———

The Baron stepped out of his nightmare chamber feeling strong and confident. His personal Killborg Attendants had scoured the city and brought him a small bouquet of alstroemerias. He held them firmly and took his private elevator to the incarceration ward.

Once the doors opened, he walked straight for Row 63, talking himself up along the way.

"This is it, Baron," he said. "No turning back now." He focused on the flowers as he stepped up to her cell.

He positioned himself and held up the bouquet.

"Prisoner Number 7, there is something I'd like to say."

But there was no one to say it to. Her cell was empty.

All the cells were empty. How long had these alarms been going off? Where were the guards? He let his arm down, holding the flowers at his side. "Well, you've blown it again, Baron."

He stepped into the space that used to be her cell and sat on her bench, contemplating. "Sometimes I think the universe wants me to be alone."

He lit a cigarette, drew deep. "They called her Prisoner Number 7, but to me, she was always Prisoner Number 1."

He sat there a few minutes, his sadness turning to anger. He let the flowers drop and left the ward.

"I'm going to man the artillery gun." he said.

———

The hangar was far from the prison riot, so its operations continued uninterrupted. Hoverbots loaded and unloaded transport craft. A few Killborg Cops waited by their vehicles, ready for dispatch. Four Guards patrolled the floor, carrying buzzsticks.

Mina, Justice, Number 1 Man, and Manborg did their best to be quiet and invisible as they moved amongst the empty boxes and cargo piled at the back of the hangar.

"Look, the bay doors are open," whispered Number 1 Man. "At last, some luck."

Justice smiled. "Yes! And see outside, that's the Multilane. It leads everywhere, we just need to find something to ride."

A constant chorus of whirs, whines, ratchets, and clicks rose from Manborg's motors and servos. Mina spoke through clenched teeth. "You've got to be quiet."

Manborg stopped moving.

Number 1 Man pointed toward a parked row of two-seater hoverbikes. "Right there. Those are what we need."

Everyone found places to hide and took in the landscape between their positions and the hoverbikes. It was only about ten steps, and the two nearest guards were facing the other way.

Justice eyed a path with some crates he could move behind. "I'll go," he said.

"How do you get them to hover?" asked Manborg. It was far from a whisper.

"Hush," said Justice, softly. "And it's just a hover-converter."

"Be quiet," whispered Mina.

The guards were no longer facing the other way. "What was that?" one said.

Justice reached behind him, smacking Manborg's leg. "Nice job, drongo!"

"Will you two shut the fuck up?" hissed Mina, hitting them both.

Twisting handgrips, the pair of Killborg Guards sparked their buzzsticks. With slow steps and careful eyes, they moved toward the cargo area, searching for the source of the noise.

Everyone ducked. Manborg's elbow tipped over one of the boxes he was hiding behind. When he tried to right it, his component-laden hands didn't cooperate. He ended up hugging the box to keep it close.

The Guards looked right at him. "Come out of there," one said.

Manborg froze. His blinking lights illuminated the space around him.

"We can see you," said the other Killborg.

"Nope," said Manborg.

"Yes, we can totally -" the guard stopped talking mid-sentence and twitched for a moment. He fell forward, revealing Mina standing just behind. The guard had two blades jammed deep in his head.

Before his partner could call for help, Number 1 Man dislocated his jaw with a *shock punch.*

Ignoring his injury, the Killborg lunged with his buzzstick. Number 1 Man deflected the stick and broke the arm swinging it with a *piston of thunder.* The guard stumbled back and Number 1 Man advanced, landing blow after blow.

Justice whistled from one of the hoverbikes. "Let's get a move on!"

A *storm of knuckles* from Number 1 Man caved the Killborg's face in, ending their melee. The guards and cops on the other side of the hangar took notice and started to move.

Manborg called out, "cover your ears!" A mortar corkscrewed out of his back and launched a sonic grenade toward the far side of the hangar. His friends cupped their hands on either side of their heads as it detonated.

For a moment, there was a sound vacuum. Then, an auditory shockwave moved out in all directions from the grenade, breaking every bone and craft in a ten-meter sphere.

Manborg signaled they were clear. Mina jumped on the bike with Justice. Number 1 Man got on another, and Manborg sat behind him.

"You kicked that guy's ass back there," said Manborg.

"Of course," said Number 1 Man. "I was the one who trained him."

The hoverbikes blasted out of the hangar. Shadow-Mega and her strike team arrived just in time to see them leave.

THE HOVERBIKES RACED ALONG, KEEPING PACE WITH THE FASTEST vehicles around them. Traveling side-by-side, everyone had to shout to be heard.

"We need to get off the Multilane," said Mina. "We look too obvious."

"And Manborg really stands out," said Number 1 Man. "He has blinking lights."

"There's no need to worry yet," said Justice. "Maybe they don't know we escaped."

The Multilane was surrounded by electronic billboards. Every one of them flashed red and displayed images of Mina, Justice, Number 1 Man, and Manborg. A mechanical voice read the words scrolling under the pictures again and again: "Citizen Alert! Armed and Dangerous Criminals have escaped from Genesis Tower!"

"Where can we go?" asked Manborg.

Number 1 Man thought for a moment. "We've got to head toward the old Hinnom District."

"No way," said Justice. "It's hours from here, and we need to hide right now. Besides, it's haunted."

"Sorry, Bro. It's a good idea," said Mina. "Our pictures are all over Meganet now. Hinnom is isolated and abandoned. We'll have a better chance of laying low."

"In about fifteen kilometers, we can head east on Malphas Court," said Number 1 Man. "That road is deserted. No patrols."

Warnings triggered in Manborg's view. He scanned the lanes behind them for trouble. "Problems are coming," he said. "Five contacts. Too far for me to target, but they are closing fast."

"How did they know?" asked Justice. Then he had a realization. "Oh crap. These bikes must have trackers."

With a shift of his head, schematics of both bikes overlayed Manborg's vision. Justice was right, there was a tracking device implanted just below the brake assembly on each of them.

Through his eyepiece, Manborg watched strings of code pop on and off, then the trackers went dark.

"There were trackers," said Manborg. "They are disabled now."

"I've always liked you Manborg," said Justice.

"I hear sirens," said Mina. Spinning red and blue lights were gaining on them.

"The ones behind us don't need trackers," said Number 1 Man. "They've seen us."

"We can't let them follow us," said Mina.

"They are already following us," said Number 1 Man.

"Then we can't let them live," said Manborg.

Justice rolled out the pistol on his right hand. "Less chatter. More splatter."

He brought his pistol around and Mina leaned left. Justice fired blindly behind them. "Did I hit anything?" he asked.

A billboard stood shattered, spewing sparks and smoke. "Yes," said Mina. "You hit something. But it wasn't chasing us."

Justice punched the keypad below the handlebars. A rearview matrix projected onto his windscreen. "That's helpful," he said.

Their five pursuers came into range. Three were Killborg Cops, darting around traffic on their hoverboards. The other two were skeletal monsters with chain guns implanted on their arms. They didn't have legs. Instead, the torso melded into a four-wheeled base outfitted with sirens and lights.

"Crikey," said Justice. "Boner Buggies."

"These hoverbikes don't have weapons systems," said Number 1 Man.

"I do," said Manborg. He reached back as his pulse cannon locked into place. He blasted it in a tight arc at the Killborg Cops, but they were too nimble and dodged every bolt.

Justice tracked his shots on the windscreen projection as he fired over his shoulder. Mina held one of the handlebars, helping him steer. With a few adjustments, he hit one of the Boners in the chest with four consecutive rounds.

Each pulse bolt tore a bloody gap into the beast. With so many chunks missing, its spine failed. The buggy veered over the center rail of the Multilane into oncoming traffic. The Boner was still shrieking as it got caught up in the axle of a carryall.

Number 1 Man kept his hoverbike weaving, dodging a stream of bullets. Two of the Killborg Cops moved up on the right and left, trying to flank the bike. "Stop your vehicle," they said.

"Nope," said Manborg. A cylinder pushed out of each hip.

CHEMICAL NET ** *ONLINE* ** *ENGAGED*

The cylinders lobbed tight balls of chemically treated microthreads at the Killborgs. Once they made contact, the microthreads burst outward, forming a caustic net. Cries and steam rose as the threads ate their way through everything they touched. The cube-shaped remains of both Killborgs scattered across the lanes.

The last Killborg Cop came up alongside Mina. He smiled at her as he lined up his pistol.

She smiled back. Before he pulled the trigger, Mina swept her hand toward the ground, and four blades pierced the Killborg's boots. They cut the energy converters, and his hoverboard disappeared.

So did his smile.

The Killborg fell at full speed and the asphalt ripped off one of his legs. He didn't have time to scream as he skipped down the Multilane, losing velocity, skin, and bone with every bounce.

The remaining Boner Buggy almost tipped over avoiding him,

and Justice used that moment to pump a dozen rounds into its wheelbase. The buggy jabbed into the road and flipped forward, decapitating the Boner before the whole rig burst into flame.

Wreckage buried the Multilane. Traffic was backed up for kilometers.

Up ahead, Justice and Number 1 Man turned their hoverbikes onto the Malphas Court exit and headed east.

For the third time, The Baron lifted Doctor Scorpius off the floor and tossed him across the observation deck. Then he leaned on the Doctor's crutch.

"So disappointing," said The Baron. "Shadow-Mega reports that repairs have been completed in the incarceration ward. All prisoners accounted for. Many are dead. The rest have returned to their cells."

He threw the crutch at the Doctor. "All but four! Prisoner Number 7, Manborg, and … those other guys. Gone!"

With measured steps, The Baron left the room. "So disappointing," he said.

Doctor Scorpius stayed on the floor. He moved his tongue around his teeth, tasting blood and taking inventory. He looked to the doorway, waiting for a crew of hoverbots or Killborgs or worse to rush the observation deck and continue his beating.

No one came. He listened for footsteps, but only heard the heavy gears of the elevator carrying The Baron to the ground floor.

It took both arms to guide his crutch into a position that allowed him to rise to his knees. There was a flutter across the operation monitors along the east wall. Scorpius tried to swallow.

"I know you're here," he said, standing. A thrumming came from all around, pressing on his head. "Whatever you're going to do, do it now. It won't matter in the end anyway."

The monitors formed a patchwork of images that combined into a single subject: a pair of dark, deep-set eyes.

"Mankind has survived worse than you!" said Doctor Scorpius.

From the dark intersections of the walls, thin tendrils lashed out and wrapped the Doctor's wrists. They pulled him tight, forcing him to drop his crutch.

He hung there as the strands pushed themselves through his skin and pierced their way along his veins and nerves. More of the tendrils snapped around his ankles and neck, burrowing into his bones and brain.

He felt tugging inside. Extraction.

The voice of Count Draculon came from all around. "Hope," he said. "You have hope, Doctor. I can taste it." Sparks flew from the equipment in the room. The dark eyes on the monitors grew brighter as the tendrils dug and drained. "I will take it from you, Doctor. I will take *all*."

Doctor Scorpius felt himself falling away, saw glimpses of the other side. "We've survived worse!" he cried. The tendrils pushed deeper and lapped up the last of him. Bolts of energy darted around the observation deck, combining into brilliant flashes, then a blazing light.

From a distance, the deck's main window shone like the sun. Nearby structures cast long shadows. Then the room went dark.

Two minutes later, the overhead lights stuttered back on. The devices and screens booted up and returned to their normal functions. The Doctor's crutch was the only evidence that anything happened here. It had fallen behind a bank of processors.

A place no one ever looked.

It would stay there, unnoticed, forever.

———

Number 1 Man lead the way down Malphas Court. "I know a place we can go. A place to provision and plan."

It had been over and hour since they'd seen anyone along the road, Hellborn or human. There were no other vehicles, no billboards showing their pictures. The dark surrounded them;

power didn't work this far from the center of Meganet City. Their hoverbikes were the only source of illumination for kilometers.

Everything they passed was broken. Fallen buildings. Wrecked transport. This is what happened in the remote districts. The human populations never stopped shrinking. As people got used up, regions emptied. Then they were demolished.

Mina saw a glow to the west. It was the remains of Sheol, the sector where she and Justice grew up. Flame Crews took it down years ago. *How can it still burn?* she thought.

Watching the road and rubble passing by made her want to doze. She drifted back to the pack of teenagers she and Justice ran with in Sheol. Their parents had been drained years before, so they lived on the streets with half a dozen kids in the same situation.

They learned to work as a unit. Any juvenile on their own either got scooped up by a Killborg Patrol or kidnapped for the black-market blood trade. But with a group, you could see them coming. Mina, Justice, and their crew learned where to hide.

After a while, they learned how to fight. They trained, and stole, and trained, and attacked the blood traders as they tried to snatch their friends off the street. Then they trained and stole some more. This went on for years.

Mina had a same-age friend in that crew, Lucy. They were a set, never apart.

Until they weren't.

The whole gang was taken into custody about two years ago. They weren't in the middle of some big score or wiring a Cop Transport to explode. They were just eating some tinned fruit they found. And without any warning, a squad of Killborgs surrounded them.

They had been under scrutiny for months, part of a new program. The Terroropticon would activate soon, and The Baron needed to populate it with fighters. Every sector got scoured for candidates, and this lot fit the bill.

Half of them died during "training," a series of elimination matches with weapons-laden hoverbots. Mina, Lucy, and Justice made the cut.

They were sent into the arena, and they did well. Not only did the crowd go nuts for these kids, but their victories gave hope to the other combatants.

But a while ago, a year? Less? They took Lucy. No explanation, no words at all. The laser barriers in front of her cell dropped and two Killborgs dragged her off, and that was that.

She didn't return. Months passed, and everyone thought they'd killed her. Then, Mina saw her again. She was leading a group of guards through the ward. Leading them, Killborgs, and she didn't say a word to Justice or Mina. They called to her, and she didn't even blink.

They did something to her. Something really screwed up. They called her "Shadow-Mega." Whenever she got the chance, Mina still called her "Lucy" or "Bud," like she used to.

But she never got a response. Lucy was either buried too deep or missing entirely.

Still, when Mina looked in her eyes, sometimes, like earlier today at that security door, sometimes Lucy came through those pupils. The way she pulled her hair behind her ear when she was thinking. The way she dug her heel into the floor when she was frustrated.

Things like that let Mina know that this was Lucy, once. And it gave her hope that, maybe, there was still a little bit of Lucy left.

———

As they entered the ruins of the Hinnom District, Justice saw the brake lights glow on the other hoverbike. "Oy!" he said, moving alongside Number 1 Man. "Are we stopping?"

"Slowing. There's a gap to the right up ahead. Then it's one more kilometer."

Small campfires burned here and there in the rubble. A few

people were gathered around them. They stared as the bikes passed. "Crikey," said Justice. "Look around, will you?"

"I know where we are," said Number 1 Man. "No one will harm us."

"That guy's got garbage on his head," said Justice. "I've heard about places like this. Are they gonna eat us?"

"You are being a ninny," said Number 1 Man.

They made the turn and stopped a kilometer later. The tiny road ended at a large field of debris. It was good to get off the bikes and stretch. Manborg scanned the area. "Contacts all around. They are human. No weapons, looks like they are hiding."

"All I see is trash," said Justice.

Number 1 Man stepped up to a twisted collection of rebar. "That's all you're supposed to see." He pulled the steel rods and two meters of debris moved with them, revealing a tunnel. "Pretty good, huh?"

With smiles all around, everyone stepped toward the entrance. They were stopped by a flurry of rags and hollering. A little person, holding a spear and dressed in a homemade ghillie suit, leapt out of the tunnel. He brandished his spear and blocked their way.

"Wailee wailee waillee wallah!" he cried. Number 1 Man approached him slowly.

"It's okay," said Number 1 Man. "It's me. Look, it's just me."

The little person adjusted the goggles that obscured most of his head, then lowered the spear. He smiled and hugged Number 1 Man.

"Wah! Gleeper peelnik Noomber Un-gahn!"

"Yes," said Number 1 Man, "These are my friends. Justice, Mina, and Manborg." The little person gave them a nod and waved them toward the tunnel.

"Crikey," said Justice. "You are one adorable little guy. I want to pet you!"

The spear came up again. "Never mind," said Justice, "Just kidding. Don't eat me or anything …"

The "little guy" stayed by the bikes as everyone else ducked into the tunnel and headed down.

———

"I can help us see," said Manborg. His shoulders became incandescent. He lit the way as they walked nearly 200 meters, then the tunnel opened into what used to be an underground storage unit.

"Thank you, Manborg," said Number 1 Man. "You can turn those off now." He strapped some wires to a solid-core power supply and a row of bulbs hanging above provided light. The place was big, but it wasn't empty. Stocked shelves lined the walls. Supply crates were stacked all around. Manborg's shoulders powered down.

"Whoa! Where did you get all this stuff?" asked Justice.

"This is where I stayed ... when I escaped," said Number 1 Man.

Justice grabbed a blue box off one of the shelves. His eyes lit up. "All right! Tasty treats! You're a life saver Number 1 Man."

"What if they find us?" asked Manborg.

"They don't patrol here anymore," said Mina.

"We will be safe," said Number 1 Man. "People have been hiding in Hinnom for years."

Justice found a chair beneath the light. He turned his head to speak to the group but stopped short. He flinched as he pulled his collar from his neck.

"You're bleeding," said Mina. She went to him and lifted his jacket away from the wound.

"It's just a scratch," said Justice. "Damn Boners."

"We've got to clean this up," said Mina. Number 1 Man tossed her a red case.

"Here," he said. "You'll find topical solution towelettes and an Amrita Collar in there."

Mina dabbed up enough of the blood to see that Justice was right, the wound was superficial. She bent the collar back and forth until it started to glow then hung it around his neck. "Is that better?" asked Mina.

"Yeah, I'm fine," said Justice. "I was fine before."

"You should rest, Justice," said Number 1 Man. "You are injured and that was a long ride. In fact, we should all rest and make some sort of plan."

"We can't just sit around," said Mina.

"I don't think there's another choice," said Number 1 Man.

Mina grabbed a handful of protein biscuits and headed up the tunnel. "I'm going to check on the bikes," she said. Number 1 Man watched her go and wondered if he should run after her.

No, he thought. *She needs a moment alone.*

"What's her problem?" asked Justice. "Ah, who cares? Let's eat!" He must have been feeling better. He had a blue box in each hand.

———

As Mina surfaced from the tunnel, she saw the little guy pacing around the hoverbikes, singing to himself. He spotted her and froze for a moment, then snapped to attention. She approached, smiling, and offered him one of the protein biscuits. "You don't have to be on guard," she said.

He took the biscuit and smelled it, then clutched it to his chest as his mouth formed a big circle with excitement. He darted off into the rubble, and Mina quickly lost track of him. She laughed for the first time in many days.

She sat on one of the bikes and ate a whole biscuit in three bites. She started a second, but took this one slower, reading the label as she chewed.

A breeze made some soft creaks in the surrounding rubble. But there was another sound rising, a low thrumming that hurt her head. She dropped her snack as the tone rolled into a baritone whisper.

"Mina," it said. She knew that voice. They hadn't run far enough.

It spoke again. "Mina … you are alone."

"No," she said. She heard metal twisting behind her. She spun around and watched as tattered wires, jagged steel, and rusted pipes gathered to form Count Draculon's visage.

It said, "Yes, you are alone. But you have … hope. So much hope."

With the smallest of moves, she readied two blades in each hand.

The scrap Count leaned toward her. "You think you can save her?" it said. "Come and face me." Then, whatever held the wreckage together vanished along with the sounds. The pieces of metal dropped in a pile, leaving Mina and her blades without a target.

She holstered the knives, then dug around the hoverbike's saddlebags until she found a pen and pad. She scrawled out a note and secured it to the windscreen.

Then she jumped on the other bike and sped off toward the Genesis Tower.

———

"No, Justice," said Number 1 Man. "It says 'four.' Four cups of water."

Justice held the blue box closer, scrutinizing. Number 1 Man pointed at the text on the back. "That's what it says - right there," he said.

With his finger, Justice traced the words. "Four. Cups. Water. Yeah!"

Number 1 Man put a pot of water on a hotplate and powered up the burner. "And then, you bring it to a boil." Justice reached over with the box.

"… add noodles," he said.

"No!" said Number 1 Man, blocking. "Not yet. First, we boil the water."

"Oh," said Justice, returning his attention to the directions. "Yeah, says it right there. Small print, as always."

"Manborg," said Number 1 Man, "shall we prepare a helping for you?"

"No thanks," said Manborg. "I'm not hungry. I don't think I eat."

"I understand," said Number 1 Man. "There is a door back there, it leads to sleeping quarters. You can rest."

"Yeah," said Justice. "You should duck off for a kip. Or a recharge or a fuel up or whatever it is you do. It's been a long day."

"Thank you," said Manborg, heading through the door. "I'll do that."

The weak burner took its time heating the water. Number 1 Man worked out with his nunchakus as he waited. Justice went back to his chair and became contemplative. "Hey, can I ask you something Number 1 Man?"

"You can ask me anything Justice. I am a friend."

"Why did you ... run?"

Number 1 Man took a deep breath and finished his nunchakus form. As he walked toward the weapon's storage case, he said, "I was given a choice: Train their soldiers or die."

With practiced care, Number 1 Man folded a cloth around the nunchakus and stowed them away. "The Baron had been watching me in the arena. He saw me using techniques his Killborgs did not possess. He also knew I was training the other prisoners, trying to elevate both skills and spirits."

"You sure helped me," said Justice. "Mina, too."

"Yes ... Mina." Number 1 Man pulled a bundle from one of the crates and shook it. It snapped into a camp chair. He sat next to Justice. "They didn't want me to train an army of prisoners. So, they made me train their army of Killborgs."

"We thought they took you away to change you. Like Lucy," said Justice.

"No, not like her. They said they would kill me if I didn't obey, but first they'd kill you. And Mina. And everyone I'd ever spoken too."

Number 1 Man showed Justice the barcode tattoo on his wrist. "I agreed. They gave me this, it told the Killborgs not to attack me. It doesn't work anymore. I trained guards and cops. I taught them everything they know."

He leaned toward Justice, and whispered, "But I didn't teach them everything *I* know."

Justice nodded. "You wily bastard. You had a plan!"

"Yes. I taught them solid fighting methods, but only those I could counter. They learned different styles of fighting, but not superior ones. They *looked* impressive, but there was no heart." He stood and walked to the burner.

"This is nearly boiling, won't be long now," he said. "One day, The Baron gave me a new assignment. I was to train his personal guard until they were able to beat me. He'd know they were ready when I was dead. When he told me this, I made a decision, right there."

"That's when you took his eyes?"

"Yes. With a *crane-pluck,* I pulled the right one out and showed it to him. Before he screamed, I repeated the move, and I had an eye in each hand. The western hangar was close, so I tossed his eyes at his feet and ran there. I stole a goods transport and fled. To Hinnom, where I was raised."

"That's where all this stuff came from?"

"Not all of it. Hinnom is home to many people. They know how to stay low, how to acquire what they need, and they share it. This is one of many communal storage areas."

"So," said Justice, "they know you. That's why they didn't eat us."

"No. Stop saying that. No one is going to eat anyone." Number 1 Man looked into the pot. "Justice, I was going to come back and save you. Save Mina. But they caught up to me in the city before I had the chance."

"Number 1 Man," said Justice, "I'm not in a cell. Neither is Mina. We *are* saved."

"I suppose you are right," said Number 1 Man. He felt some of his shame evaporate. "The water is boiling. Let's finish making this delicious meal."

9 / TURNING AROUND

The progress bar in Manborg's view finished filling in. As it vanished, the words "All Systems Optimal" appeared and then faded away. "Are they really, though?" he said.

There was an alarming cracking noise underneath him. The cot he'd been sitting on could no longer support his weight. He stood and leaned on the wall instead. He popped open the storage cubby on the back of his hand and took out the photograph Wayne gave him, all those years ago.

As he looked at his old self and his brother, he tried to remember more. What did they sound like? Where did they live? The details were absent.

He heard a clacky shift from his cubby. The future-cassette Doctor Scorpius gave him fell out onto the floor. He tucked away the photo and picked up the tape.

It was old, the label was beat up. As he was looking at it, his eyepiece flashed.

*CASSETTE RECOGNIZED ** Open tape drive? (y/n)*

"…yes?"

There was a buzz and clatter as a tiny door slid open on Manborg's side. He dropped the cassette in and closed the door.

*TAPE DRIVE ** BOOTING ** RUNNING - scorp.ai.prj*

One of his processor lights glowed brighter than it had before. It projected a beam, and that beam took on the shape of a person.

It spoke. "Hello Manborg. You remember me, don't you?" Though blue and translucent, the figure was unmistakable. "It's your old friend, Doctor Scorpius."

"Hi," said Manborg.

"Quiet, I'm talking," said the hologram. "If you're watching this, then chances are I'm already dead. Or worse!" The doctor shook his fist. "That also means it's time to fight. To send these soulless invaders back to hell and save mankind!"

"You got the wrong brother," said Manborg. "I'm not a hero."

"Calm down, Manborg, I know what you're made of. I hid your body away and used their robo-technology to create the ultimate warrior. The Count's power grows with each passing hour, but so does yours. The only one who can stand against him ... is you."

———

An armored Killborg Cop stopped its hoverboard on a corner outside the Genesis Tower Complex. It spoke into a walkie on its shoulder.

"This is TQ 835 to control. I've finished the perimeter sweep, there's nothing out here."

A speaker in the Killborg's helmet responded. "Then go around again. Find something. Find someone, anyone, I don't care. We need to look busy. I've never seen The Baron this mad."

"All right," said TQ 835. "I'll bring in the next pedestrian I see. We'll figure out what they did later. Signing off." The cop looked up and down the street, but there was no one in sight. Then a thin blade severed its spine while another pushed under the rim of the helmet and into the back of its brain.

After it hit the ground, Mina withdrew her blades and cleaned them off on the Killborg's sleeve before she holstered them. She heard heavy steps coming, so she dragged the body behind a column and hid there.

A Bug-brute crawled by. It was in a hurry, headed for the tower's entrance. These were a new form of Killborg, with six motorized legs, capable of climbing a vertical surface. She might have a chance to sneak in after it went through.

She skipped two steps in that direction, then a grate opened under her feet. She fell in, and the grate closed above her.

———

"One of our hoverbikes is gone," said Number 1 Man, "and I don't see Mina anywhere."

He and Justice had finished their meal and brought a plate up for her.

Justice threw the plate. "She's been eaten!"

"I told you to stop saying that. We need to look for her."

A piece of paper waved on the windscreen of the remaining hoverbike. Justice grabbed it. "Number 1 Man, I found something," he said.

"What is it, Justice? A clue perhaps?"

Justice recognized her handwriting. "It's from Mina."

"Yes ... yes?"

It says ..." he tugged at the edges of the paper. "Just one second." He turned the page sideways and brought it closer to his face. "Should've worn my glasses."

"Perhaps if you let me ..."

"Oh, who cares what it says! She's gone!" Justice tossed the note and Number 1 Man snatched it out of the air. He studied it aggressively.

"My god," he said. "It's suicide!"

"What?"

"She's returned to the Genesis Tower, to the arena. She's going to fight ... Count Draculon." Number 1 Man let go of the paper.

"Mina," said Justice. "Why? Why would you do this alone?"

"How can we save her?" asked Number 1 Man. "We can't fight an army on our own."

Justice grabbed him by the shoulders. "If you care about her," he said, "you'll do it."

"How?"

"I'll tell you how," said Manborg. He'd been listening from the tunnel's entrance. He walked across the debris field and joined his friends. "We go in there ... and we kick some ass."

"Manborg!" cried Justice.

"That's quite the proposition you have there, Manborg," said Number 1 Man. "What if we're too late?"

"It's never too late - to be a hero," said Manborg.

"You're bonkers Manborg," said Justice. "I love it! Let's go!"

Manborg's tape drive spun, and the holographic Doctor Scorpius addressed the group.

"Hang on," he said. "Manborg needs to work with me, just for a short while, to become completely battle-ready."

Justice and Number 1 Man didn't know what to make of this translucent version of their former enemy. "What's that traitor doing here?" asked Number 1 Man.

"He died," said Manborg. "This is a pretend version of the doctor. He left it for me. Doctor Scorpius is the one who attached all this stuff to my body so I can stop Count Draculon."

"I'm more than a 'pretend version.' This is the most advanced exercise in whole brain emulation ever achieved," said Holo-Scorpius.

"Doctor, why does your hologram still use the crutch?" asked Number 1 Man.

"Please, enough questions, we need to train," said Holo-Scorpius.

"It's a good point," said Justice. "I mean, you could have working legs, a jetpack, and four arms if you wanted, right?"

"Maybe I didn't think of that, okay?" The hologram was losing patience. "Maybe when you're quietly creating a holographic future-cassette in secret, hoping they don't find it and kill you for your trouble, maybe you get in a hurry and leave out some of the fancier options like customizing your avatar!"

"Sorry," said Justice. "Just asking. No need to get cranky."

———

Manborg raised his arm, deep in thought. "Don't fire, just extend," said Holo-Scorpius. With a small shift of his wrist, Manborg's pulse cannon locked into place. It hummed as it powered up. "No," said Holo-Scorpius. "Don't power it up. We're striving for control. Just draw the cannon then put it back."

The canon powered down and folded away. "I think I've got it now," said Manborg. He held out his arm, and rocked it to one side, rolling out the pulse canon. Then with a twist, it locked away. He repeated the sequence twice more. "Excellent," said Holo-Scorpius. "Now try it with a target."

Some twenty meters away, the little guy had set up a row of cans along a board. Manborg lined them up in his view, then rocked out the pulse cannon and fired. The first blast tore the board and all the cans to pieces. Then he tucked the weapon away.

"Very good," said Holo-Scorpius.

———

Justice had painted fresh stripes on his cheeks. He used alternating, well placed shots to keep an old bucket in the air over his head.

———

Manborg extended his blade and Number 1 Man raised a wooden sword. They moved through a series of sparring exercises. "Your skills with that blade arm are much improved," he said.

———

The little guy set up another row of cans. Manborg stood ready with his arms at his side. "Concentrate," said Holo-Scorpius. As soon as the targets were ready, he said, "FIRE!"

His eyepiece flashed, and Manborg saw each of the six cans highlight. He swung around his rail pistol, and it racked six shots in less than a second. All the cans flew off into the darkness.

"Holy mackerel," said Holo-Scorpius.

————

At the hoverbike, Justice and Number 1 Man checked all its functions. Holo-Scorpius spent a few moments making certain Manborg's connections were tight.

"Your power is beyond anything the world has ever seen," said Holo-Scorpius. "But the greatest power of all is deep within you." He tapped Manborg's chest. "Down in your core, you've got a cylinder of liquefied Amrita Life Source. In its normal form, it can heal a wound, or sustain the infirmed."

The hologram looked skyward. "But I distilled it, concentrated it. This version of Amrita cured a death." He turned back to Manborg. "Your death. That's why they can't stop you. And the distillation secrets died with me, so you have the only batch of liquefied Amrita Life Source the world will ever see."

Manborg touched his chest. "That's pretty cool."

"Yes," said Holo-Scorpius. "Way cool."

————

Justice, Number 1 Man, and Manborg hopped on the hoverbike. Holo-Scorpius stood with the little guy.

"You've got a lot of killing ahead of you," said Holo-Scorpius. "Good luck."

"It's not about the killing," said Manborg. "It's about family." He looked to Justice and Number 1 Man. "We're a family now."

They sped away on the hoverbike as Holo-Scorpius and the little guy waved and cheered them on.

Justice looked back, thinking. "Manborg," he said, "if you're not projecting it, how can that hologram exist?"

"I don't know," said Manborg. "Do you want to go back and ask him?"

"No," said Justice.

———

Thanks to Mina's reflexes, she went limp and tucked on the landing after she fell through the grate. She got a bruise on her hip, and it took a minute to get her lungs working again, but that wasn't a lot of damage.

She sat on the floor, taking in her new location. Shafts of light came through staggered grates like the one she had dropped through, creating light pools here and there. She saw some of the details of the chamber, but beyond those bits of light, there was only darkness. There might have been a wall, or a passageway, or open space that went on for kilometers. No way to tell.

Chains hung from the ceiling. Many had hooks on the end, and many of those hooks had bits of flesh hanging on them. The smell of wet rot choked her worse than the fall.

Terrible things happen here.

She got on her feet and put a blade in each hand. She sensed movement behind her and hurled one of the blades as she turned. It flew into the darkness and clattered on the stone floor.

She hadn't hit anything, but then a kick to the back of her head confirmed she wasn't alone down here. She spun and brought the other blade forward, too late. Another kick landed on her ribs, and she was on the deck. Again.

With slow and confident steps, her attacker walked into the light pool and looked down on her.

"Hey, Bud," said Mina, coughing.

JUSTICE HAD DISCONNECTED EVERY SPEED LIMITER AND POWER restrictor on the hoverbike. The trio could barely hold on as Number 1 Man barreled down the Multilane toward the Genesis Tower Complex.

"Oy, Number 1 Man, jam on that accelerator," said Justice.

"On it," said Number 1 Man.

"And Manborg, jam their scanners," said Justice.

"On it," said Manborg. "What are you doing, Justice?"

"Me? I'm getting ready to jam."

———

Shadow-Mega raised her boot, intent on smashing Mina's head. Before the boot came down, Mina did a log roll and got clear. She sprung to her feet and hurled another knife. Shadow-Mega twisted to elude the blade. She was a fraction late and caught a nick on her cheek.

"Lucy, I won't kill you," said Mina. "But if you're in there, I may have to hurt you to break through." Another high kick just missed Mina's head. She was outreached if Shadow-Mega kept using her legs, so she had to get in close.

She charged, one hand ready to punch and the other ready to

stab. Shadow-Mega moved back, looking for the advantage, but Mina kept advancing, keeping the space between them tight. Mina took little steps at angles off her center line, creating opportunities for a punch or slash.

No more throwing knives. If she backed up far enough to allow for that, she'd get kicked again.

After a few rounds of thrusts and blocks, Mina finally connected with a strong lead hook, dead center on Shadow-Mega's ear.

As Mina followed through, Shadow-Mega pounded her elbow into Mina's side. It felt like getting hit with a club. Mina was off-balance, and before she could recover, she got kicked to the floor again. She landed on her belly, facing away from her opponent.

Mina heard the slow steps coming toward her. She was about to get stomped. She closed her eyes and timed her breathing with the footfalls. At the right moment she spun on her hip and powered a blade into Shadow-Mega's ankle.

An inhuman cry left Shadow-Mega's lips as she reached for the blade. Mina sprung off her hands and smashed both feet into the center of Shadow-Mega's chest, driving her into the darkness.

Standing, Mina called after her. "You don't have to do this. It doesn't have to be this way, Bud."

Nothing.

Mina tried again. "Let me help you," she said.

She heard wet, tearing sounds and a low growl. Shadow-Mega emerged from the darkness. She wasn't human at all. She was three times Mina's size, with a thick hide housing bunched, ropey muscles. She roared and raised her massive fists over her head.

In that moment, Mina realized her friend had died months ago. Lucy wasn't coming back.

———

On the lower processing floor of the Genesis Tower, the Bloodscrappers had their hands full. Dozens of prisoners from the riot had been killed and, per protocols, their corpses had been drained upstairs at the drawing stations. That process captured the purest blood.

From there, the bodies came to the Bloodscrappers' floor. The scrappers used their specially designed rollers, presses, blenders, emulsifiers, and centrifuges to get every molecule of plasma out of the remains. Killborg Guards patrolled the floor to make sure the Bloodscrappers weren't stealing sips or smuggling.

With every machine on the floor running, nobody noticed the glowing orange spot in the center of the south wall. It was heating up and starting to dissolve due to an onslaught of plasma energy from the other side.

Once the heat became palpable, two of the guards moved toward it to investigate. A barrage of flash missiles tore a clean hole in the wall and spattered the guards all over the room.

The hoverbike soared through the hole. Manborg, Justice, and Number 1 Man jumped off and let the bike crash into one of the main pressing areas, wiping out the six Bloodscrappers working there.

"Sorry for crashing your party," said Justice. He took the east side of the floor, snapping his arms like a traffic cop as his pistol shots ripped through his soulless targets. Every round struck with startling accuracy.

Manborg took the west side. His pulse cannon dispensed impartial destruction. Bloodscrappers, machinery, lighting fixtures, and guards were all torn to bits in equal measures.

Number 1 Man ran at the larger guards one-at-a-time with his nunchakus whistling. The weapon struck each one with enough force to knock their heads clean off. He hammered his way to the room's only entrance and disabled the locks with a savage *specter kick*.

They had the room cleared in three minutes.

"I've blocked the door," said Number 1 Man. "They can't get in that way."

Sirens were coming from outside. "Yeah," said Justice, looking at the hole in the wall. "But we made a new door, remember?"

"On it. Cover your ears," said Manborg. Two sonic grenades brought the wall down on the Boner Buggies coming through the hole. It was all rubble now, no one would be getting in that way, either.

As the sonic waves rang out, Manborg heard Count Draculon's voice, riding them.

"Come to me … keep your promise," he said. With the voice came knowledge. Manborg knew where to find the Count.

He stepped over bodies and rubble on his way to a hatch. "Oy," said Justice. "Where do you think you're off to?"

"Go. Find Mina. Save her," said Manborg. "I've got a score to settle."

Justice didn't feel good about splitting the party. "What did you say about us being a family? Families stick together!"

At the hatch, Manborg ran the code to hack the lock. Programming and instinct drove him. He was built for this purpose. "I'll see you all soon," he said.

"No! Manborg don't go in there!" cried Justice. "That sign says 'danger!'"

Manborg looked at the sign over the hatch. "It says - 'ELEVATOR.'"

Justice looked harder and sounded the word out. "El … ah … vay … elevator. Right, okay. Off you go."

Manborg gave Justice and Number 1 Man the same awkward thumbs-up he showed after their first battle. The hatch rolled open and Manborg headed up.

Number 1 Man put his hand on Justice's shoulder. "You'll see him again," he said.

"That'd better be true," said Justice.

———

In this brute form, Shadow-Mega was a lot tougher. She was also slower, easier to dodge. But if those giant, clawed hands connected with even one good thump, Mina was dead.

The beast left itself open frequently, allowing Mina to punch, kick, and slice, but she didn't do much damage. She was getting tired, and the creature was just getting started.

As they fought, they had moved through the chamber. Mina noticed it was brighter here than where they started. A glance upwards showed her why: The grate over their heads was missing.

She had found a way out.

Shadow-Mega swung at her again, expecting Mina to repeat her pattern of punches and stabs. Instead, Mina ducked and slid around the creature's back. With her next step, Mina pushed off the wall, then the beast, then the wall again, gaining height with every jump.

On her next move, she vaulted off Shadow-Mega's head and leapt out the opening above, slamming one of her knives all the way down into brute's skull. The monster screamed, flailing at its wound, trying to remove the blade.

On the surface, Mina saw smoke and sirens around a broken wall at the base of the Genesis Tower.

———

The elevator doors opened onto the observation deck. A familiar, low thrum greeted Manborg's ear, but this time it wasn't from the electronics. The source was tendrils, dozens of them extending from every dark place in the room. They quivered and writhed, like living things.

Someone stood in front of the main window, his back to Manborg, looking out over Meganet City. All the tendrils terminated in that figure. Some in his wrists, many in his chest, a few around his neck. Manborg's scanners showed fluids pumping through the tangle.

Fluids being forced into Count Draculon.

He'd grown larger since their last meeting. He was swathed in thick, spiny plating. It was impossible to tell whether the chitinous layers were armor or an exoskeleton.

"I was hoping we would meet again, Manborg," said the Count.

"Is that what they're calling you now?" He gathered several of the tendrils in his fist, feeling their pulse. "I've changed as well. The rich blood of combatants, from this Terroropticon, it flows into me. Makes me strong."

The Count's form didn't matter to Manborg. He had a singular purpose. "You killed my brother," he said.

"I killed everyone," said Draculon. The tendrils snapped away and withdrew to the darkness as he turned to face Manborg. "So, take your vengeance."

"Oh yeah!" cried Manborg. He raised his pulse cannon and charged, but before he moved one meter or got off a single shot, Draculon lifted his hand and hit Manborg with a blast of pure, dark energy. Manborg's systems went haywire just long enough for the Count to toss him out the window of the observation deck.

As Manborg fell, his armor reconfigured. He'd be able to absorb the next energy blast. He landed, hard, in the center of the arena. The crowd was louder, more out of control than ever before.

His systems quickly recovered. As he stood, he saw the source of the crowd's adulation.

Count Draculon was floating from the observation deck to the arena floor, pumping his fists over his head and driving the fans wild. He was on every screen in the Terroropticon.

He was on every screen in the world.

———

"Maybe we should have gone the other way," said Justice.

He and Number 1 Man were hemmed in behind a boiler, surrounded by Killborgs. They had cleared most of the tunnels beneath the Bloodscrappers' floor, but there was still no sign of Mina. Their last turn brought them to this concourse, where two squads were gathering to hunt them down.

Their arrival saved the Killborgs a lot of searching. Now they were under heavy fire.

"Look at them, Justice," said Number 1 Man. "They are holding their positions, just as I trained them to do. They think this formation gives them a strategic advantage. If I can create a path, you can hit them where they stand."

"You taught them to stay still? You're a genius, Number 1 Man!"

"Be sure to keep in motion. They have trouble hitting moving targets."

"Just wait until they see my moves," said Justice.

Number 1 Man spun his nunchakus and leapt from their hiding place. He took down a nearby Killborg with *the lemur's smile,* a form he'd never shown them. The other Killborgs held their places and clocked their weapons toward Number 1 Man, but he had already moved on.

Another guard's chest folded in as the nunchakus struck. Then Number 1 Man jumped over him to disembowel one more with a *gunpowder palm strike.*

Justice dove out from the boiler and landed on his feet. He danced and spun along the path Number 1 Man created, blowing away the Killborgs all around them. He'd worked out a firing solution and as long as the Killborgs stood obediently, he'd have no trouble taking them out.

When their numbers dwindled to six, the Killborgs changed their tactics. They fired on the run. "Great," said Justice. "We're down to the troublemakers."

Number 1 Man was no longer on the offensive, it was all he could do to dodge the pulse bolts. Justice fired wildly and managed to blow out two of the Killborgs' faces.

That was the gap Number 1 Man needed. A *kicking gale* knocked the nearest guard to the floor, and a *drunken llama elbow* crushed its skull.

The last three Killborgs put their shoulders together and launched a barrage of pulse bolts that sent Justice and Number 1 Man leaping for safety again. They landed behind a long cart. "Now what?" said Justice.

The cart was getting shredded by the Killborg's pulse rifles. "We can't stay here and there's nowhere to go," said Number 1 Man.

One of the Killborgs let go of its rifle and shook with a spasm. Another one froze; stopped moving altogether. The last one kept firing but yelled at the others. "What's wrong with you guys? We've got them pinned!"

Mina popped up behind him. "Pretty sure you're the one who's pinned," she said, driving a knife in through his eye and out the back of his head. The other two Killborgs fell over. Blades protruded from the base of their necks.

"Mina!" said Justice. The group gathered.

"You're alive," said Number 1 Man.

"Damn right," said Mina.

A small, titanium cylinder flew in and clattered on the floor between them.

"Concussion grenade!" cried Number 1 Man. Everyone leapt out of the way as the device exploded, sending a shock wave and flames out in all directions.

Mina hopped up first, shaken but unharmed. "What the hell?"

"I'm okay," said Justice. "Thanks for asking."

Number 1 Man had a scrape on his shoulder, but that was all. "Where did it come from?" he asked.

"Crap," said The Baron. He stood at the concourse entrance. "Nice one … how do you miss with a grenade?!" He threw another.

Number 1 Man spun his nunchakus and knocked the cylinder away. It detonated clear on the other side of the room.

The Baron pulled an ordinance belt out from under his coat. He fumbled to get another grenade out of its pocket. "You know," he said, "I'm over you, Prisoner Number 7. I've given it a lot of thought, and I can't be my best self when I'm with you."

Before he had the next grenade in hand, Number 1 Man tackled him. They both tumbled backwards through the entrance and the hatch closed behind them, leaving Mina and Justice alone.

"Don't worry," said Justice. "He can handle himself."

Mina looked past her brother and saw trouble. "I hope you can say the same for us," she said. Justice followed her gaze and saw

Shadow-Mega walking toward them, blood streaming down her face.

She had not been able to extract the knife. All her efforts only managed to drive it deeper into her skull. Her injuries left her unable to control her chimeric DNA. She kept convulsing between her Lucy form and her brute form, or a twisted combination of the two.

———

Working the crowd, Count Draculon faced Manborg with his arms outstretched, inviting him to make the first strike. Manborg held nothing back.

He pumped out his entire supply of chemical nets, sonic grenades, and flash missiles. The arena shook as the Count was enveloped in explosions, smoke, and flame.

Manborg's systems targeted Draculon inside that blazing cloud. He fired his plasma beam, rail pistol, and pulse cannon simultaneously. He kept the assault going until the weapons overheated and shut themselves down.

All went quiet as the smoke cleared.

The Count remained standing with his arms outstretched. The chemical nets had left a herringbone pattern etched into his armor but other than that, he was untouched. Flourishing his cape, he walked a small circle, showing the crowd he was whole.

The arena erupted with cheers.

Manborg ran through his checklist:

PULSE CANNON ** *offline* ** *cooldown*

PLASMA BEAM ** *offline* ** *cooldown*

RAIL PISTOL ** *offline* ** *cooldown*

FLASH MISSILE ** *offline* ** *stores empty*

The Count locked his eyes on Manborg, waiting to see his next move.

SONIC GRENADE ** *offline* ** *stores empty*

CHEMICAL NET ** *offline* ** *stores empty*

One weapon left, the first one Manborg ever used. He'd trained on it with Number 1 Man, it might be enough.

The pneumatics triggered, and a long silver blade extended from Manborg's forearm. A smile crept across Count Draculon's face. "Yes," he said. The Count snapped his arm out to his side, and a lengthy, jagged sword appeared in his spiked hand. "Let's begin."

11 / ALL FALL DOWN

Sparks and flames crawled up the walls around Number 1 Man and The Baron. They were in one of the main generator rooms, part of Meganet City's vast power grid.

The Baron squirmed out of Number 1 Man's hold and jumped to his feet. He adjusted his gloves, revealing backplates dotted with pyramid spikes on each hand. He threw off his long coat, uncovering a tapestry of similar armor and points underneath.

An inventory of styles and forms ran through Number 1 Man's mind. The Baron knew more than his thugs, so choosing a method would be just as important as its execution. He brought his right elbow to eye-level and his left foot forward.

His left arm came around with tremendous force and introduced The Baron to *the hare's relentless bite*.

———

It didn't matter where Justice shot her, Shadow-Mega kept getting closer. Head, center mass, kneecaps, the pulse bolts struck but barely penetrated. He'd moved ahead of Mina, hoping to shield her, but it wasn't looking good.

Shadow-Mega got right in front of him, and for the moment held her brute form. He kept firing into her face as she reached out and pitched him into the wall. He dropped to the floor, unconscious.

Mina held her largest blades in each hand and sprinted at the creature.

———

The relentless attack knocked The Baron back, but he was still on his feet. It should have been fatal. The two of them began trading strikes and blocks. Hard.

"You're good, Number 1 Man," said The Baron, between punches. "But I've upgraded. Not just these new eyes, but my skin and muscle as well. You are now obsolete."

Number 1 Man shook his head. "The power of the human spirit will never be obsolete."

The Baron let out a sigh. "No surrender then? All right." His fists shifted higher, and he rushed Number 1 Man.

———

The blades clashing in the arena rang and sparked. Between Manborg's programming and his training with Number 1 Man, he managed to block every move Draculon made. But he hadn't got a hit in, either.

Twice, Draculon had used his free hand to fire dark energy at Manborg, but neither attack caused the devastation he was expecting. The Count's frustration was building.

Manborg's other weapons remained in stasis. For now, this exchange of swords was the only option.

———

The fierce blur of his hands proved The Baron had indeed upgraded. The specificity of his attacks kept Number 1 Man on defense.

He blocked The Baron's *mantis shrimp thrust* with a *comet's sweep*, and in that moment Number 1 Man realized he'd used an inferior counter. He'd left himself open. "Fool," he whispered. "I am sorry, Mina."

The Baron saw the opportunity and brought down the *demon's two-fisted maul.*

The form was known only in legend. All a defender could do was brace. The blow sent Number 1 Man sledding across the floor. He was unsure exactly where he was struck, the pain burst outward from every cell. He focused on his breathing. Focused on recovering his abilities. Focused on staying alive.

The spasms and needles were still ricocheting inside Number 1 Man when The Baron reached down and wrapped one hand around his neck. He hoisted Number 1 Man up. His feet were left dangling as his face met The Baron's.

"We gave you a chance to join us," said The Baron. "To become something more than just a man."

Number 1 Man stayed on his breathing. He felt his ears pounding. "I am more than you'll ever become, Baron."

"Did your pathetic human desire make you throw it all away?" The Baron slammed Number 1 Man to the ground. "It wasn't love, was it?"

Number 1 Man sprang to his feet, damaged but ready for more. "Yes."

"Oh." The Baron softened his posture. "I see. You know, I was in love once. Rips you apart …"

An opening! Number 1 Man had completed the breaths necessary to charge up his next attack. He thrust his hand forward, two knuckles protruding, and rapped the center of The Baron's sternum.

"No," said The Baron. By the time he moved his arm to defend, the next five strikes had already pounded targets around his shoulders and thighs. In the following second, a series of punches smashed nerve centers on The Baron's neck, ears, and temples. Number 1 Man had executed the *seventeen points of still waters.*

The Baron stood helpless. The form triggered paralytic neuropathy, preventing all movement. But Number 1 Man knew it would not last.

He planted a *mule kick* into The Baron's pelvis, bending him in half as he flew across the room. He straightened out again when his spine slammed into an open energy conduit on the opposing wall.

His body crossed the circuit, and he became a power conductor for the Genesis Tower. He shrieked, still unable to move as the electricity boiled his insides. His upgraded skin and muscle tried to contain the energy until, with an unholy cry, he exploded. Number 1 Man was showered with The Baron's remains.

He brushed the larger pieces off, then ran through a fissure in the wall created by The Baron's demise.

———

Shadow-Mega's chimeric DNA stabilized, but she'd stay in her brute form forever. The knife in her head was pushing on her left eye. It bulged nearly out of its socket. The monster was half blind, all she saw was rage.

Mina was dodging and slashing as before. The creature's swings were wilder, harder to predict. A glancing backhand put Mina on the ground, three meters away.

The beast staggered toward her as Mina tried to find her breath. She heard a groan; Justice was starting to come around. That was when she noticed The Baron's ordinance belt laying near her brother. The Baron must have dropped it when Number 1 Man tackled him.

It was labeled "GRENADES."

"Hey! Justice!" Mina yelled.

Justice rolled to face her. "Eh?"

"Grab the -" Shadow-Mega stepped on her chest, slowly crushing the life out of her. She could no longer speak. Her hand pointed frantically.

"What?" asked Justice. He looked where she pointed and saw

the belt, but the writing made him pause. "Crikey, need to sound this out. Gee ... Are ... Backwards three?"

Mina managed a scream as one of her ribs popped. Justice pulled it together.

"Grenades," he said. "It's grenades!" He ripped one of the cylinders off the belt and leapt to Shadow-Mega's face, taking her by surprise. He jammed the explosive into her mouth.

"Less reading, more bleeding."

Shadow-Mega stumbled one step back and Justice dove near his sister.

"Too ... close ... dumbass," Mina gasped. They shared a smile, clasped hands, closed their eyes, and waited for the explosion.

Number 1 Man sprinted in from across the way. He sent Shadow-Mega farther down the hall with a *gull over the water* kick.

The creature managed a muffled shriek before a blinding flash and pressure wave destroyed her. As the debris and monster bits settled, Mina, Justice and Number 1 Man rose to their feet.

"That was intense," said Justice.

"Yes," said Number 1 Man.

For the first time today, no one was trying to kill them. They spent a few moments appreciating the relative stillness.

Then came the unmistakable sound of cheering from the Terroropticon.

"Now what the Hell is that?" asked Justice.

"It's got to be Manborg!" said Mina.

———

When it seemed the series of slashes, parries, and fades would never cease, Manborg finally drew blood. He made a perfect feint, and the Count, lulled into thinking his opponent was tiring, left himself open, just for a second. Then Manborg swung high.

He cut a small gash across Draculon's face. The crowd shared a gasp as The Count stepped back and touched the wound. The arena floor lapped up the drops of foul blood and ichor that fell from his cheek.

Mina, Number 1 Man, and Justice arrived at the arena's edge through the prisoner's entrance. The Killborg Guards had abandoned their posts to watch Count Draculon fight. "Woah," said Justice. "Looks like our boy Manborg has this handled!"

Count Draculon held his bloodied hand to the crowd. "Clumsy of me," he said. The crowd laughed and cheered.

"Time to end this!" shouted Draculon. He turned to Manborg as everyone in the Terroropticon chanted and stomped:

"END HIM! END HIM! END HIM!"

With a clutching motion, the Count caused gaps to appear in the ground near Manborg. Flames leapt up, there was no way to retreat.

"Hell yes!" cried Manborg. "Let's end this!" He lifted his blade arm and charged at Draculon. He'd drawn blood, and it empowered his rage. It erased any advantage his training or sensors gave him. He slashed again and again, out of control.

Draculon easily anticipated Manborg's attacks. After a few exchanges, he waved his free hand, sending a small flash of dark energy into Manborg's face, blinding him for a moment. In that moment, the Count brought down his sword, and cut off Manborg's blade arm just below the elbow.

Vision returned to Manborg just in time for him to see his human hand and its sword mechanism clatter at his feet. Vitality fibers hung from his stump, spilling preservative stabilizers.

With every system reeling, Manborg dropped to his knees.

"We've got to get in there!" Mina shouted. Justice and Number 1 Man tried to hold her back, but she broke free and ran toward the battle.

Draculon held Manborg's head in his hand and pressed his sword against his neck. "Prepare to meet your brother in Hell."

Mina stopped running, there was no more time. She threw her largest blade with every drop of hatred and hope inside her. "Prepare to meet this!"

The knife spun end over end as it sailed across the arena and through the flames. The point struck Count Draculon dead center between his shoulders and pierced his armor. It dug in clear past the grip. He jerked, grunted with pain, and released Manborg's head.

The chanting in the arena ceased as the Count spun around to see Mina. "Mina, you made it," he said. "Welcome." His eyes drew tight as he sent a plow of dark energy at Mina. It carried her four meters before it dissipated, and she dropped.

She wasn't moving.

But Manborg was. His systems had recovered. The mechanical fingers on his right hand clamped down on the remains of his sword arm, creating a single, makeshift unit.

The Count had his back to him, so he called out. "Draculon?!" The Count didn't think he'd ever hear that voice again. He turned to Manborg, curious.

"More like 'Asshole!'" cried Manborg, and he drove the blade clean through the center of Count Draculon's throat.

The Count choked words through the blood clogging his mouth. "You cannot kill me," he said.

With a savage twist and pull, Manborg tore the blade sideways through Count's neck. Draculon's head lolled over. It was still held on by a scrap of demon flesh. He fell to the ground, but somehow, he was laughing. "You cannot ... kill ..."

His eyes drifted to the growing red area that surrounded him, and his laughter stopped. The arena floor was an astringent construct, designed to draw in and capture every drop of blood spilled there. There was a rush of red and black fluid being pulled from the Count's neck.

"... no ..."

As Count Draculon was drained, so was the power that held the Genesis Tower together. The Terroropticon creaked and shifted. Sections of the stadium fell. The crowd tried to flee, trampling each other.

In less than a minute, Hell's ruler on Earth had become a brittle husk. That dry, hollow shape collapsed on itself as did everything around it.

———

Manborg's only thought was getting his friends out of there. He used an arm and a half to carry Mina out of the arena as it crashed around them. He joined Number 1 Man and Justice, and together they ran clear of the flames and falling debris.

They found a small rise, away from the chaos. Justice and Number 1 Man tossed enough rubble out of the way to make room for Manborg to put Mina down.

"She took a hit of pure electron energy," said Manborg. His eyepiece glowed as he completed a medical scan. "Instantaneous cardiac arrest."

"My sister's dead?" said Justice. "We have to do something."

"There's nothing we can do," said Number 1 Man. "She's gone."

"No," said Manborg. He accessed his inventory and brought forward all the information he had on his liquified Amrita Life Source. "I have something inside me that can help."

The armor on his chest shifted. Two of the plates moved aside, exposing a glowing blue cylinder. Justice started to speak, but Number 1 Man put a hand on his shoulder, and he remained quiet.

Manborg took the cylinder from his chest and poured its contents into Mina's mouth. All waited, and after a few seconds, her eyes went wide. She drew a deep breath and sat up.

She was alarmed, but alive.

"Mina!" said Number 1 Man.

Justice giggled.

Mina smiled at everyone. "What happened?" she asked.

"We won!" said Justice.

Manborg fell over and lay on his side. The others gathered around him.

"Manborg," said Justice, "don't tell me that chest serum stuff was all you had."

"It was," said Manborg.

"You're a hero, Manborg," said Number 1 Man.

One of Manborg's processor lights grew bright, and a voice cut through the darkness.

"Hello Manborg," said Holo-Scorpius. "Hello everyone."

"Hi," said the group.

"Yes, it's me Manborg," said Holo-Scorpius, "and I have someone here with me who wants to say hello."

Holo-Scorpius looked to his side and another hologram appeared next him. It was Wayne Halloran, still in his combat gear.

"Hey bro. It's me. Remember, I died way back when? Just wanted to say you did great out there."

This brought smiles to everyone.

"Oh, one other thing," said Wayne. "There's no heaven."

Manborg's smile dropped. The others looked at each other, puzzled.

Wayne stood there smiling while Holo-Scorpius motioned for him to go away. Finally, he took the hint and left.

"Goodbye Manborg," said Holo-Scorpius. He walked off, talking to Wayne "I swear, are all big brothers assholes?"

The system monitors in Manborg's view tracked his rapid deterioration. One by one, processes were shutting down. "No heaven?" he asked.

"Just let go, Manborg," said Justice. "Is there a light or something?"

Manborg's eyepiece flickered and went out. He went limp. Complete system failure.

Justice, Mina, and Number 1 Man stayed with Manborg for a time, not sure what to do next. Then, the tall hill of debris that was once the Genesis Tower let out a rumble.

Dozens of Bug-brutes, in a vicious parade, poured out of the top. They were followed by squads of Killborg survivors, looking to even the score.

Justice locked his pistols into place. Mina fanned out six blades in each hand. Number 1 Man raised his fists. They knew what to do next.

The three of them charged at the hill without fear, because they had a weapon that made them undefeatable.

They had hope.

Whether you saw Manborg in a theater or in your home on VHS, Blu-ray, DVD, or streaming, hopefully you stayed through the credits. Because after the credits there was an extended trailer for another film.

The producers of this novelization would be remiss to exclude Bio-Cop from these pages. So, included here for the first time anywhere, are the lyrics to the first track on the unreleased Bio-Cop soundtrack album.

THE BALLAD OF BIO COP

It's a classic tale of hate and crime
and acid blood and dermal slime
in a city plagued by junk that they called DRUGGZ.

Nothing known could get you higher.
The Super Burly Bros were suppliers
The cops made war against this bunch of thugs.

One brave cop tried to infiltrate
the warehouse where the DRUGGZ were made.
The signs on building said that they made rugs.

He snuck in through a window
and he found a bunch of shelves
with chemicals stacked way up to the top.

Then an unexpected earthquake
dumped them on his head
and that's how he became BIO-COP.

(chorus)
BI-OH-COP
Pain receptors on overdrive!
BI-OH-COP
Doesn't even know why he's alive!
BI-OH-COP
Justice can never die,
with BIO-COP on our side!
(end chorus)

He drowned in a scientific stew
His skin became a deadly fondue
In a nonstop drippy gore and blood ballet.

The doctors didn't know what to do
with a man who excreted caustic goo
then a secret science group took him away.

They said "Here's a cop they cannot kill
but he can kill by standing still
and coughing up a foul corrosive spray."

They assigned him to a precinct
and gave him a badge and gun
to catch the Burly Bro's and make them pay.

BIO-COP kept screaming,
"Why am I alive?"
He tried to die but failed, every day.

(chorus)
BI-OH-COP
Pain receptors on overdrive!
BI-OH-COP
Doesn't even know why he's alive!
BI-OH-COP
Justice can never die,
with BIO-COP on our side!
(end chorus)

Then those Super Burly Bro's created
their own mutant thug.
A BIO-PSYCHO killer dressed in chains!

He battled BIO-COP for days
and in the end,
both mutants found a friendship formed in pain.

This misshapen pair is still at large
Causing Mayhem is the charge
There are warrants out for them in twenty states.

With BIO-PSYCHO behind the wheel
BIO-COP can finally feel
something more than agony and hate.

He's found a friend, and friends are really great!

(chorus)
BI-OH-COP
Pain receptors on overdrive!

BI-OH-COP
Doesn't even know why he's alive!
BI-OH-COP
Justice can never die,
with BIO-COP on our side!
(end chorus)